With best wishes —
Tracy ♥

THE UNHEIMLICH MANOEUVRE

THE UNHEIMLICH MANOEUVRE

Tracy Fahey

Boo Books

Published by
Boo Books
32 Westbury Street
Derby
DE22 3PN
boobooks.net

Introduction © Cate Gardner 2016
All stories © Tracy Fahey 2013-2016. See copyright acknowledgements
for first publication dates.

House cover image by Judy O'Riordan
Cover design by Daryl Duncan
Typesetting by handebooks.co.uk

ISBN 978-0-9954551-3-9

Printed in the UK

CONTENTS

INTRODUCTION

In her own words, Tracy Fahey describes the *Unheimlich* as stories of the uncanny (the uncanny domestic to be more precise). Unfamiliar with the word Unheimlich, a quick visit to google translate led me to scary, eerie, uncanny, sinister, weird, creepy, spooky… The tales within are certainly uncanny and a little off-centre. These are stories of ordinary people with seemingly ordinary lives, tales that are classic in form and yet set very much set in our modern world. Many end with the traditional twist in the tale, with some of the stories starting after the event has occurred and looking back, protagonists telling us what happened to them, how they came to be there, of their damage.

I first met Tracy at a book launch for an anthology in Manchester back in 2013. After the event, a group of us went to a pub to chat about the event and about writing in general. A good evening and only a need to catch the last train home drew us away. I recall Tracy telling us about the ghost estates in Ireland, where only a few of the homes were occupied and some of the building work had stopped leaving completed houses next to empty shells. Tracy visits these estates in her story, appropriately titled, Ghost Estate, Phase II. Ever since that meeting, I've been haunted by the idea of these empty streets.

This collection opens with a dream-like story of a girl waking from a coma and ends with a story about the protagonist's childhood dreams and her grandmothers distorted memories. For me, the stand out story was *The Woman Next Door* a tale about a new mother who is struggling to cope, thinks she isn't good enough and fears she will lose her partner, possibly to her perfect neighbour, another young mother, the perfect mother. The stories are all told in the first person in a world you and I would recognise. They are stories of folk who take the wrong road, knock on the wrong door, and find themselves somewhere not quite right. The real world surrounds them but it seems they are unable to turn the corner and return to it. They are lost now.

Tracy is a student of the gothic, and the stories within *The Unheimlich Manoeuvre* are quietly gothic. I believe this edition is to feature interior photography by Tracy. I look forward to matching the images to the stories.

You've possibly picked up this collection because you're already familiar with Tracy's stories or perhaps you are new to Tracy's work, one of those delightful readers who are willing to take a chance on a new writer, and Tracy is just that. Tracy is a new writer, and it is an amazing achievement to have a collection published so early in her career. She is a writer finding her voice and there is a flow to the stories within, they fit together. Now go read her stories of doppelgangers, of ghostly estates, her tales of the modern gothic.

Cate Gardner
Wallasey, June 2016

COMING BACK

My world ended precisely two months ago. I awoke from a coma to find myself gone.

I'm in a strange bright room and someone is shouting at me. I strain to move my head. There is a hard plastic mask fastened to my face like a hideous carapace. I claw at it weakly, bones like water, eventually managing to knock it aside. My hand falls, exhausted. Something is wrong. I squint. My arms are splayed, like Christ crucified, with one, two three, *four* tubes poking out. *What's happened?* I try to croak, but my mouth is ashen, cracked with thirst. Intense weariness smothers me, utter and boneless. A doctor stands at the foot of my bed. She is rude, squat and froglike. She barks at me 'You stupid girl! Didn't you know you were sick?' Possible words muddle together, stick in my dry mouth. I can only look at her, stupidly. My brain blunders inside my skull like a moth in a darkened room.

I am in a waking sleep; I see people pass by my bed. Their faces blear and swim as my eyes slip closed. When I open them, I see a blonde nurse, her hair a halo under the fluorescent tube. I know I must look terrible, a tangle of machines and untidy flesh. I try to joke, but the words jumble and slur. She looks at me. I see her brisk kindness in her eyes. She takes my wrist. I clutch her hand. It is warm and solid. I fall into sleep again, down the dark tunnel. Coming back I see the angry doctor making notes on her clipboard. I open my mouth to tell her I'm sorry, but I'm gone again.

Words keep penetrating. 'Coma' – I have been in a coma, they say, over and over again. I don't remember. I know I have been away. I am sick they tell me. Very sick. I have undiagnosed Type 1 diabetes. There is a lot of information about blood sugar. They show me insulin pens. It is too much. There is nothing in my head except a fuzzy blackness. I gaze down. I am wearing unfamiliar pyjamas. I have no idea how I got them, or who put them on me. I don't want to know what happened to my slack, lifeless body in the emergency room. It was not me. Like a large, strange baby, I lie in bed; my waxwork-self fed, sponged, injected. Drugged up, half-waking, I live in a perpetual swoon. I am a ghost in the machines. I sleep at an angle, arms outstretched, tubes pushing nutrients into the soft marshmallow of my arms.

All over the small ICU, worlds end, softly, one after another. The man beside me keeps coughing. I can't sleep. He coughs on and on, his breath tearing at his throat between bouts. I am almost hysterical with rage. —*Stop!* I yell inside my head. I roll my head hard from side to side in anger, one of the few movements I can make. But he doesn't stop. The wet, tearing sound goes on and on. Behind the curtain I hear more and more murmuring. The door of the ward opens, closes, then opens again. In the morning the noise has stopped. The curtain between our beds is still drawn, but the visitors have gone. 'I'm sorry,' says the blonde nurse gently, as she rearranges my sheets. 'He passed away in the night.' I am quiet. A small, mean, part of me enjoys the new silence. Otherwise I feel nothing.

Emotions have drained out of me, like urine down the catheter that lies warm against my leg. (I have no idea how or when they attached it, my brain flails away from the very idea. The thought of having it removed makes me shrink into the sheets around me. I am afraid of more pain.) All I want to do is lie in bed and doze off, again and again. The only thing that rouses me is the sight of a needle. Then I cry and beg, drawing my arms as close to me as I can with the tubes knitted into my skin. The tender crook of my left elbow flowers with appalling roses of red, black, yellow, blue, a horrid clustering of repeated punctures, fingerprints, incisions, invasions.

People come in to visit. I find it hard to remember them. I am *too tired*, the nurses fuss, too tired for visitors. There is a sister, and a father. They both have dark hair and seem familiar, yet not, all at the same time. They stand like statues, sadly looking down at me. Sometimes one of them will cry. They bring me things, fruit, water, books. For the first time in my life, I can't read. I look at the pages and the words crawl around each other. I know I was away and the world ended. That is all. My stomach tells the tale of my journey back, livid with injections, a map of reddened and bruised flesh.

Sometimes I wake and there is a man by my bed. He arrives at night, but never by the main ward door. From time to time I will see a golden spill of light fall from behind the nurses' desk on the furrowed linoleum of the floor. He steps out into the dim, hushed light of the ICU. Often he will walk up and down, looking at the four beds in the ward. I don't know what his name is; in my head he is the Visitor. He only sits beside my bed. I don't mind. He sits quietly, large dark eyes fixed on my face. At first, he says nothing, just looks. There are no questions, no tears and no needles. It is strangely relaxing. He doesn't wear a white coat, or a nurse's uniform, just a nondescript brown suede cardigan. This makes me like him more. One night he lifts a lock of my hair up to examine it. 'You could change it, you know.' They are the first words I have ever heard him speak.

'Why?' I am intrigued.

He looks at me coolly. 'Because you're not the same anymore.' He is the first person to say it. I stroke my hair and nod. 'People like you, who become so severely ill, often find it difficult to remember things. Don't try; it's a good kind of amnesia, death amnesia.' I like that phrase, sounding it silently in my head. He nods at me. 'You're not the first to go away. But you're one of the first to come back here. You have to change now.'

'Why?' It seems to be the only question I can ask.

'Your old world is over. Forget about it. If you want to fight, to keep going, stop trying to remember.' There is a low groan from one of the other beds. He looks over his shoulder, then back at me. 'You know what I mean, don't you?'

'Yes.' I think I do. I close my eyes. When I open them, he is gone.

That is our longest conversation. He comes back again, but only at night, only when the ward is quiet. He offers me advice – 'Stop trying to remember. It can't help you now,' sometimes even praise – 'You look stronger,' but he refuses to answer my questions, even the one that plagues me, *who am I?*

Now I can walk. I can pretend. From time to time I smile at people when I realise it is appropriate to do so. I arrange my face in a listening attitude when they speak. I hold myself together tightly. If I unravel, I am afraid someone will find me out. I am hollow.

The worst bit is when they move me to one of the main wards. Everyone tells me this is a good thing. It feels like leaving the only home the new me knows. I shrink from the strange smells and noises of my new environment. There is still a wall of greaseproof paper between me and myself, both transparent and opaque. I can remember a misty before-time, I can remember the ambulance, the repeated questions, opening my mouth to tell them my name, but the words going the wrong way, falling down the back of my throat. Then nothing. 'Tell the man I'm going,' I say to the nurse. She is properly confused.

'Who?'

The Visitor I think, but can't say. Hesitantly I say, 'The man who comes at night.'

I sound like a child. Her face clears, 'Oh, you mean Pat, the night nurse? Not a bother, of course I will.' I keep quiet. It is not Pat. Pat likes to read tabloid newspapers and drink tea, and even, sometimes, to sleep behind the nurses' station when everything is quiet. The other man does none of these things. The nurse pauses, raises a finger in the air – 'Wait!' She disappears behind her desk, and then returns with a large, shabby black handbag. I look behind her. The wall behind the station runs smoothly, with no surface deviation. The door out of the ward simply isn't there. I shake my head, confused. My eyes keep doing this, playing tricks on me. Some days my vision doubles, blurs. Some days I see moving specks out of the corners of my eyes. 'Here, it's yours.' The nurse holds out the bag. 'Thanks,' I mumble and drop it on my trolley. I push the heavy trolley slowly ahead of me to my new bed, placing my unsure legs one after the other, all the way down the corridor. I don't look back.

In this ward, I am no longer special, no longer tended by the calm, antiseptic nurses of the ICU. The nurses here are rushed, hardy, terrifying. 'How do you do this again?' asks a nurse, casually squirting excess insulin from the needle as she reads the instructions on the cardboard box. She pinches a fold of my stomach and injects me with a quick stab. I whimper slightly. 'Now don't be like that,' she chides. 'Sure, look at the wee size of that needle. It won't hurt you.' She is maybe five years younger than me, but she has the brisk, bossy tone of a much older woman. The mint-green paint on the walls is chipped and stained. For most of the day I pretend to be asleep, only waking to eat or stare at the ceiling. I feel well enough to be bored. I want to see my Visitor. He is the only person who talks to me like an adult. But he doesn't visit me in this ward. Maybe it is because there is no demarcation between day and night here. I am in a room with two old ladies with severe respiratory problems. They smell of old clothes and, disturbingly, of urine. 'We don't sleep,' one of them gargles at me, almost proud. Nor do they. Night after night, they sit up like giant squatting birds, watching old movies, the staccato gunfire of westerns or the mawkish syrup of Hollywood violins providing a soundtrack as they breathe noisily behind their grim respirators. I take to wandering the green-lit corridors, scratchy-eyed and exhausted. 'Where are you going?' they caw in unison as I slip past them.

Homesickness gathers thick in my throat, like throttled tears. I want to go back, but I don't know where back is. The handbag reveals some clues. I search it carefully, laying out all my possessions on the bed, and then shaking the bag gently to make sure nothing has lodged in the crevices. There is a paperback horror novel, *The Dead Zone*, as well as a Kindle. *I liked to read*, I think, wistfully. There is a tattered notebook filled with scribbling I find difficult to read. Most pages are covered with plans about work – dates of meetings, endless to-do lists. I can dimly remember the large red-brick building I work in and the smell of waxed tiles in the corridor on Monday mornings. Faces of colleagues pass through my head when I see their names. The problem is no longer that I cannot remember; it is that I feel nothing when I do. This scares me slightly. Some of the scrawled entries are diary-like scraps. I read until my eyes blur, but I don't understand them. I discover that I like Japanese food – *really? Isn't that mostly raw fish?* I also seem to watch a lot of horror movies, something that I cannot believe I will ever do, or want to do again. My smartphone is an even better source of information. I've charged it up and keep its settings switched to silent, as I watch the number of missed calls mount up, steadily, day after day. Messages continue to buzz through, concerned, sympathetic, and then filled with a kind of frustration. 'Please text back. You know I'm worried about you.' I don't really know who they are. No-one is as worried about me as I am. I don't reply. I am more interested in the photos I find on it. I look at the photographs of my careless self, face cracked in a great smile, hair blowing in the wind, surrounded by an endless pageant of buildings, landscapes, people. Sitting in the hard hospital bed, I cannot remember what it was like to feel so enthusiastic. There is even a video of me making a message for a friend. It *looks* like me. It *speaks* like me. It *moves* like me. I feel a wave of despair at the impassable walls between myself and myself. *If you want to fight, to keep going, stop trying to remember.*

I try, I really do. No-one told me coming back would be such a long journey. The weeks on the ward tick by. The harsh sound of the ventilators and the tinny TV keep me awake at night. I am desperate to escape. *If you want to fight, to keep going, stop trying to remember.* So I fight. I fake it. I take my sister's hand when she comes in, and call her by name. It's easy, she's told me it so many times before. I tell my father I feel much better. Both of them live at the other end of the country – I know that if I reassure them, they will stop visiting. I show the nurses how well I can I inject myself. Under it all, I cannot feel anything. I cannot let myself feel anything or I will feel everything. The tears, anger, humiliation, fear are brimming inside me. One false move and it will all overspill, tumultuous. Better to move through the days, slow and deliberate, measuring, injecting, waiting. I am a metronome. Four punctures a day. Four measurements. Four readings. Four injections. Four sets of numbers. Good numbers are five, six, seven. Bad numbers are any others, an infinite universe of possible numbers. The blood ritual hurts. My fingertips bruise, the pads of the third and fourth finger on my left hand are pocked with hard punctures. Needle after needle. Each measurement is a worry or a sweet relief, a small wedge of time that leads to the next one. Every needle prick is a reminder of difference, my new, abnormal body that must be controlled like a science experiment. This afterlife is no wraith. It is leaden, monotonous. Even the fear is cyclical. It is a new, careful world. *If you want to fight, to keep going, stop trying to remember.* I stay alive. I don't do anything else that requires effort. I measure my energy like a miser, hoarding it, doling out just enough energy to walk through each day. No more. Sometimes even lying in bed I can feel the reserves drain out of me, like water from a tap. In my head, I am forever marked 'fragile'. I handle myself with care.

One night I drift into the Emergency waiting room. I can hear voices, urgent, calling. 'Can you wake up?' 'It's very important you stay awake! Come on, good girl.' 'Did you have a fight with your boyfriend?' 'Don't cry.' Their voices rise. 'Stay awake!' I am rooted to the spot, a fascinated eavesdropper on someone else's dark moments. *Tell me more.* I sit on the cold plastic chair and wait intently for the story to unravel. There is a dull, repetitive sobbing and more cries of 'Good girl! Stay awake now!' Then there is silence, the urgent bleeping of a loud machine and the sound of a door closing. I feel a strange sense of dislocation – *Was that me?* Echoes stir within me, they flutter and almost, but not quite, become memories. I am haunted by that most terrible of ghosts, my own shadow-double.

I start to walk back down the corridor, then pause. I see a man in the distance. He is wearing a brown jacket – or cardigan? I scrunch up my eyes against the cold green light. Yes. He looks like he is the right height. My heart is beating fast. Heedless of my energy, of the slippery floor, I run around the corner, then pause, baffled. The long corridor stretches before me, empty but for a trolley bed, stripped bare apart from a lone pillow.

Even the nurses comment on my health now. 'You look lovely and rosy,' says the bossy one approvingly. 'We'll have you home any day now.' The thought is exciting and alarming, in equal quantities. I know where I live. I've seen the address written down in my own looping handwriting. I am good. I am obedient. I plot my escape, like a prisoner on the World War II movies that play on the ward TV, night after night. I am still faking it, but more and more successfully every day. Now I know the hospital, and all its crevices. I prowl the corridors. I've even found a place to sleep, a tiny visitor's lounge on the floor above me. I lie there, on the lumpy sofa, savouring the far-off buzz of noise, the slip-slop of sensible nurse shoes passing, intersecting, moving off into the distance. Sometimes I hear the urgent *wargh-wargh-wargh* of the ambulance outside, the brakes, the shouts of the paramedics. I roll myself up in the prickly woollen blanket and snatch a few hours' sleep.

It is on one of those nights he finds me. I wake up, and there he is, serene as ever, darkly outlined against the yellow glass of the internal window to the corridor. I sit up, excited.

'You're almost ready to go.' His voice sounds kind.

'Yes.' I hug my knees to my chin. 'Any day now, they say.'

I see the outline of his head nodding.

'Just remember to keep looking ahead. Keep facing the future. Don't look back. If you can see it, it can see you.'

I am confused. 'What can see me?'

'Nothing you can remember.' He touches my hand. His hand is cool and smooth. I feel the worn butter-soft texture of his cardigan sleeve. 'When one world ends, another can begin.'

And now I'm home, or in the house the old me used to live in. In spite of my Visitor's advice, I can't stop thinking about myself, my old self. *Who was I? Where did I go? Did I dream?* I walk around the house and examine all things I've loved, clothes, books, paintings, looking for clues, a way back in. *Who was I?* I don't have to work now. Being in a coma is a watertight medical alibi for taking time off. My old thoughts are gone. When I sit and think, there's a curious nothingness that almost feels like peace. Instead I look, intensely, at details around me, a glinting, frail cobweb, a smudge on a window-pane, a piece of thread coiled on the floor. Life is very beautiful and very strange. Sometimes I stir and realise evening has melted into night; the room has become so dim I need to switch on the large lamp. The yellow glow chases the shadows back to the edge of the room.

Home is not a place I am comfortable in. I move jerkily through the unfamiliar territory of my former life. The walls that surround me cannot protect me from my own treacherous body. I still sleep in jagged patches, waking, confused, alarmed at the silence, no respirators, no footsteps, no trolley trundling by. I'm still walking at night, but on a larger scale. I walk alone in the darkness, my feet tracing circles around my old ways. I walk the same paths, down my street, past the lighted windows. I consult my notebook with its lists. Here is where I went out for my last birthday. Here is where I worked. I stop at each monument to myself. Nothing. I look at the houses – such a thin shell that separates inside from outside, light from darkness. The walls keep everything outside. I am not afraid of anything outside. Sometimes I think I see him on the dark streets, my Visitor, but it is always someone else, some boy, some man, some woman. I miss his calm air. I even miss his brown cardigan.

Mostly I miss his advice. I try to remember it, and to forget what came before. I delete the photos from my phone. They make me feel inferior, like a bad photocopy of myself. Then I delete the numbers. I get my hair cut short and dyed a defiant, platinum blonde. My face gains colour. I wear red lipstick. I am cold and careful. I test, measure, inject. My doctor says I am a perfect patient. 'Gold star standard,' he smiles, pleased, as he checks my numbers. Under my calmness, I am angered by his praise. This is not a feat. This is a fight. My new body must win, every time.

The only thing I have in common with the old me is that I still read a lot. My tastes are morbid. At first I Google 'diabetes' and eavesdrop on forums. Most of them are based in the US, and are full of sad little misspelt tales of amputations and complications; there are too many former patients resting with Jesus for my liking. Instead I switch to reading endless articles about people in comas. I am especially fond of miracle recoveries. People who hear things. People who see white lights, deceased family members, even themselves, spread and helpless, far below in hospital beds. For me, in the darkness there had been only darkness. The only light was the buzzing fluorescent tube in the ward ceiling when I came back. But still I read on, avidly. Somewhere in this morass of articles I will find what I am looking for.

Sometimes I just sit and look out of the window. In spite of my Visitor's advice I slip back sometimes and wonder – *where was I?* In my body, I know; I know that I was somewhere and only part of me returned. The darkness took something from me; I'm not sure quite what. Sometimes I

19

let myself remember what I saw in the soft darkness. It was nothing I should be afraid of. It was only her after all, my old self that I lost that night. In the night I can sometimes hear her wandering around inside this new body that lies heavy as a slug on my bones. She is lost, forlorn, forever my dark echo.

If you want to fight, to keep going, stop trying to remember.

So I face forward. I fight. I keep going. When one world ends, another begins.

GHOST ESTATE, PHASE II

After what has happened, you don't cope too well. Things are ugly and strange. You live in a house full of loud voices and hot anger. Then a door slams. Silence. Nothing. The familiar things about you turn hard and hostile. Your head hurts. You forget things. You drift in an unhappy dream of wakefulness and weeping.

The only thing that makes sense is to leave. So you do. It's hard to remember *how*. There is a dim sense-memory somewhere of driving through the night, of seeing and not-seeing all at once, plastic bags jutting against your headrest, startled cars repeatedly flashing at you to dim your headlamps.

Your friend living in London offers you her house in the West of Ireland. 'Don't expect anything,' she warns. 'It'll be awful. It's in the middle of nowhere. There's no-one living there.' The house is uninhabited. It is not-there. That is enough.

It is a ghost estate. An unfinished estate. The idea soothes you. It is nowhere. It runs on nevertime. It is like a strange forest, the streets all named for trees. You live at Number 5 Willow Drive. Behind you is Birch Road. To the left is Oaktree Gardens. And so on. You feel free to wander around it, filled with a horrible thistledown freedom to float away, unnoticed, unmissed.

You're free.

You're free to cry, free to eat cold toast, free to make and forget cups of tea, free to spend hours obsessively cleaning out cupboards or staring out the window. Free to wear the same dreadful house-uniform, day after leaden day, black pyjama bottoms with worn knees, bed-socks and a thin grey sweatshirt, bobbled and soft with age.

The nights are bad. Dry-eyed, mannequin-stiff, you lie in bed, brain crawling relentlessly over old conversations, decoding the nuances of voice and speech, searching for retrospective clues. Sometimes you close your eyes for long enough for patterns to form and dance in the blackness. It is as close as you come to dreams. Lying there you intone a mantra – *Soon it will be morning. Soon it will be morning.*

Soon it will be morning. Eventually, the blind turns a paler grey, then streaks with orange, signalling the end of another night, the beginning of another day.

The days are better. Marginally. Sometimes they drag endlessly, seconds crawling, the hands of the kitchen clock stuck rigid, unmoving. Other days just slip by, morning into night, shockingly unmemorable. Sometimes you wonder – *Did I go into work?* You have a blurred memory of getting into the car, freeze-frame shots of yourself nodding hello at the receptionist, a drift of paper on a desk, a circle of blank faces around you at meetings. But *actual* memories, of feelings, thoughts, conversations? None.

There are the drives too, that eat up those lumpen hours between work and bed; long, aimless, crawling drives down grass-tufted country lanes, following the brown heritage signs to castles, old churches, ogham stones, sites of ancient battles. Arriving at your destination brings no sense of relief. You just sit in the car, unmoving. Sometimes you cry.

You like to walk around the estate. It requires no thinking. It's easier than work and somehow less depressing than the drives.

You live in Phase I, the first phase of the estate, the finished part. There are a few occupied houses. There's an old couple a few doors down, him quiet, white-haired, defeated, her pinch-faced, mouth twisted in a sneer of permanent disappointment at her neighbourhood. There's a small family in Birch Road, two children, one silent boy, one muted and strangely forlorn girl, cycling around on their tiny coloured bicycles, their wheels leaving a trail of echoes in their wake. No-one ever talks to you, waves at you, acknowledges you. Everyone is trapped inside their private house of misery. Oh, and there's also a woman you see, in a red jumper. You don't know where she lives, but you see her, from time to time, wandering up and down the paths. She is the only other person who ever goes into Phase II of the estate.

Phase II of the estate is very different. You like that part best. It is surrounded by a barricade. Leaning metal chicken-wire frames tilt against each other, balanced on half-built breeze-block walls. There are dusty security signs up – '24 HOUR SECURITY' they spell out, 'THIS AREA IS MONITORED NIGHT AND DAY' – and dirty white

CCTV cameras, peeling with rusty scabs. You ignore all of them. There is a gap between the red-brown chicken-wire frames to slide through. Inside Phase II, the houses form a strange mirror image of your own street. The houses look normal at first, but the gardens are overgrown, nested with great drifts of purple weeds. There is the intense hum of bees, the dry ticking of insects, and the faraway dimmed buzz of a car winding a slow path down the main road. You walk down the grey, pitted walkway. Flowers crawl around your feet.

Phase II is ripe with strangeness. It is an uncanny mirror of your twinned Phase I. There is even a doppelganger of your own house. Number 5 Evergreen Drive. When you press your face close to the dirty window your shadow reveals the dark scar of a fireplace, a bare concrete floor, a broken plastic chair in the corner. In the tangled garden of Number 5, someone has dragged weather-pale planks on top of two large paint buckets to form a rough bench.

You like to sit there, the warm August sunshine gilding the hairs on your bare arms, the scent of wildflowers heavy in the thick air. Sometimes butterflies unfurl from the weeds, paper-white, fragile powder-blue or colourful explosions of yellow-orange-red-black. Once you saw a dragonfly, hovering, its long body a flash of peacock blue, hanging still and somehow sinister in the air. Sometimes you dream you live on Evergreen Drive, like Sleeping Beauty, roses growing over you, over your house, over the paths. Behind you, the completed houses of Phase I mirror their uncanny doubles. *Here*, you think, *here the outside matches my inside.* It is your place.

A few streets in, and the estate grows more feral, darker, more dangerous. Half-built house-skeletons press against the sky, some windows nailed up with faded boards, others open, black, blank. The only person you've ever seen here is the woman in the red jumper. She's always in the distance, drifting along in a zigzag walk. Once your foot kicked a stone and you saw her start and disappear into the head-height weeds of an abandoned plot. She hides. Her erratic walk carries an undeniable whiff of madness. You like her, obscurely. You admire the persistence of her wardrobe. Her red jumper is the bright double of your own permanent home-uniform.

Some days you are convinced that there is another version of yourself, a better version, still living in your old life, still smiling, talking, walking, and enjoying life outside this bubble.

Some days you're almost happy.

Some days you think you'll never be happy again.

August drifts into September. The days compress, the nights swell into long, unbearable stretches of time. You buy books and fill the empty darkness with lamplight and stories, the more improbable the better.

It is a hot, muggy September night. Even if you could, it is too hot to sleep. You lie in bed, reading, your body prickling with perspiration, moving restlessly. Your knees slide against each other, damp with heat. You are queerly restless. Options flit through your mind – a cup of tea, a shower, some TV. No choices appeal. Abruptly, you stop reading, feeling feverish, querulous. You get up and look out the window. There is a full moon, almost hidden behind black trailing clouds. You stare at your reflection in the dark glass. You see your eyes, dark-ringed and weary, the slick of sweat on your collarbones. Portishead play softly on your stereo, a muffled sequence of dreamy, thrumming sonar notes sounding from some lost ghost-ship. There is a flicker of movement at the corner of your eye, a flash of colour. *Red?* A red jumper? Is she outside, walking?

Suddenly, you know exactly what you want to do. You are filled with a strong desire to stand on dew-damp grass and to rotate slowly till you catch a faint after-breath of breeze. You don't even stop to think. Outside, there is almost perfect silence, broken only by the dim low throb of Portishead drifting from your window. You walk through the estate, in the darkness. There are streetlights dotted around the estate, puddling orange light on the footpaths. Other streetlights loom dark overhead, broken and not replaced. Silently, your bare feet tread cat-light on the cool concrete paths. As you walk silent and sure, down Birch Road, you see curtains move against a lighted window. For a few seconds you and the silent little boy look at each other then, with a twitch, the curtain falls.

You keep walking. At the fence to Phase II, you pause. Beyond the wire fence darkness lies like a blanket, only the faintest shiver of moonlight glinting through the overcast sky. You stand, undecided. Then a cool breeze blows from the long grasses, as cold as if a fridge door had opened. *I know my way blindfolded* you think, confident, as you slide between the barriers.

It is cooler in these dark not-streets. Damp air ruffles your hair and blows a chill little breath up your pyjama legs. You drift on, airy in darkness, like a dandelion clock.

Abruptly, moonlight slants through an opening in the clouds. The light gleams palely on the windows of the houses. You see you are standing on Evergreen Drive. You thread your way through the weeds towards the bench in the garden of Number 5, then stop. It's not there! You turn around, bewildered. The bench has gone! And – even stranger – it looks like someone has cut the grass in the garden, inexpertly, unevenly. Is it the wrong street? The wrong house? But no, the moonlight softly illuminates the street-sign, the house door. *The door!* The faded door you are used to seeing is open. It yawns ajar, dark, cool. You stand outside for a moment. The clouds peel off the moon. Suddenly it is bright as day. You feel exposed. The door stands open, inviting. The oddest thought springs up in your head. *If I could lie down in here,* you think, insistently, *I could sleep. I could sleep in this cool, silent house.*

And you step inside. The hallway is perfectly dark, but the door opening off it to the sitting-room is outlined in light. You are finally inside the window. You look through it, the glass no longer dirty, the garden no longer unkempt. You feel a quick surge of vertigo – *which Number 5 am I in?* – then are reassured by the familiar broken plastic chair in the corner, the empty hole for the fireplace. The moonlight pours in, a limpid pool of pearly light. You tilt your face towards it, eyes closed.

There is a noise. Your eyes pop open. There it is again, a faraway sound. Something dropping? Then you hear it a familiar pattern, repeated, the patter of footsteps. With a hiss, you draw in your breath. Clouds pull the moon back into shadow. You feel yourself wake completely, like a dazed sleepwalker. The shame of trespassing jolts through you. You slip out into the hall again, hand on the door. The footsteps are louder now, more insistent. You hear the unmistakable sound of bare feet slapping on concrete. And now, too, horribly, you hear the sound of ragged breathing. The footsteps are growing closer. You act entirely on instinct and pull the door closed, hands finding the bolt and sliding it to. You run into the living room, stand flat against the wall, heart beating thick and fast in your throat.

The footsteps slap-crack up the path, louder, louder. There is a sound of a body falling against the door, hands scrabbling for the handles.

'Let me in! Oh please, let me in!' – Then terrible, tearing sobs.

The hands clatter over the wooden door. There is a thud as they hit the wall, then the sharp scrabble of fingernails on glass as they find the window.

'Let me in! Oh please, let me in!' Fists beat against the glass.

Your heart is hammering in your throat. Your body feels dream-heavy, unable to run. Unbidden, the night-mantra words come back to you. *Soon it will be morning.* The wracking sobs grow louder. *Soon it will be morning.* You wrap your arms around yourself, cold hands clutching your elbows, feeling their points jut, impossibly real, into your palms.

The screams and thumps abruptly stop. You move slowly, cautiously towards the dark window. Outside all is black and still. Nothing. You place your hands lightly on the window-pane. Then it is bright. The sharp white of the moonlight pours in. In a moment of clear horror, you see her, the woman in the red jumper.

There was a time, as a child, when you insisted on sleeping with the curtains drawn tightly. You cried if the tiniest chink was left open. It was just a dream, your parents told you, over and over, softly, then crossly. You were too young to tell the difference. All you knew was that you were in bed and someone was outside your window, trying to get in. You heard the crunch of gravel under their feet, their hands beating the glass. Night after night this dream would come. You were too afraid to shout for help. All you could do was pull the blankets and pillows over your head, to muffle the sound, to hide. You hid, and shivered over all the different things that might be outside – giants, witches, monsters.

Now you stand, flooded with terror pure and stark as ice. You're falling, sinking, everything inside you drops vertiginously in a swoon of fear. Yet still you stand, hands splayed to the glass, feeling the vibrations of the pounding. In a dreamy, half-frozen sickness you watch the fists bang again and again against the window-pane.

'Let me in! Oh please, let me in!'

When you were a child you were always afraid to go to the window. That was wise. All of the imaginary intruders you dreamed of drop away.

What stands outside, face stretched and distorted in terror is worse than any imagining.

What stands outside is you.

WALKING THE BORDERLINES

I'm writing the story of me and Charles Anderson. It's a story from the year I turned twenty and went travelling. It's a story of where we went and what came back.

My memories, inevitably, have been shaped by photographs. In the photo, he's smiling an all-American smile, the sun is shining and he's linking arms with me.

I'm sitting here, trying to remember what happened fifteen years ago.

I remember lots of disjointed things about that Parisian summer, like a recovering amnesiac. I remember huge dogs, fetid gratings masquerading as toilets, post offices like palaces, palaces like boulevards, beautiful bridges topped with cherubs, the sinister red-lit Redons in the Musee D'Orsay, and the overriding smell of the Seine – a dank, foxy smell of sun-warmed urine.

And Charles and all that happened after. It all happened. I remember it with almost-sadness; nostalgia for the person I was.

It was late afternoon beside Notre Dame, sun slanting low and yellow across the bar table. Charles and I were talking about life and death and life after death.
No, back, back further than that.

We met in the hostel lobby standing by the desk. Charles. It was a strange feeling. We smiled broadly at each other, smiled like old friends, and I felt an immediate shock of recognition. There wasn't even a desire to start talking immediately. He was standing with my Irish backpacking friends Sam and Adele and we all started chatting. Finally, inevitably, I turned to him.

The next bit is a montage of the lobby, the street outside, the bar, the bar table, his pack of Marlboro lights, his soft

Alabama accent, our conversation.

'He's nice, isn't he?' Adele asked.

'Yes,' I agreed.

But how did I really feel about him? Even back then, that first night, I had that inflated, giddying feeling when you meet someone you click with, when you can think of nothing more intoxicating than becoming the friend of this new, fascinating person.

The next day we went to my 'usual' café, Le Chat Noir. It was late afternoon beside Notre Dame, sun slanting low and yellow across the café table. Charles and I started talking about life and death and life after death.

'Do y'all believe in an afterlife, another dimension?' He cocked an eyebrow at me.

'Well, I do think that there are more things in heaven and earth, Horatio…' I began my pat answer, and then stopped, recklessly. 'Actually yes, I've had weird things happen to me – I've heard and felt things I can't explain.'

He nodded peacefully

'I mean *really* strange things. Once in college, some friends were messing around with an Ouija board at a party. They started screaming about someone moving the board. I thought it was just a ploy to get attention, until I heard a strange noise, like a group of people whispering in unison. I didn't even think. I just acted.'

My voice grew smaller. I snatched a quick look at his face to gauge its expression. He continued to nod, slowly.

'So I put my palms on the table and started saying the Our Father, over and over. All around me I could hear people calling to each other. Under my hands I could feel – I don't know – a kind of a thrumming.' I searched for words. 'Like when you put your ear to an electricity pole as a kid. I kept saying it – some people joined in – and then, suddenly it was over.' I sat back in my chair, remembering. 'Funny thing is, no-one ever mentioned it again. But I lost a few friends that night. People don't like it, it turns out, if you think you hear noises from another dimension. Strange, that.'

I sneaked at look at him from under my eyelashes. He touched my hand.

'S'all right now.' His voice was soft as syrup. 'No need to make a joke of it. Folks are just afraid of what they don't know. There's more than you, you know. I call them border-liners. People who can see or feel things like you. '

I looked straight at him, eyes wide.

'Why do you say that?'

'Because I'm a borderliner too.'

I sat there in the warm sunshine, looking at his blue, una-fraid eyes. In another world, close by us, everything ticked onward, the buzz of voices continued to sound around, a car horn blared, two dogs barked in quick succession. At our table, there was nothing else but our conversation.

'Tell me about you,' I urged. 'I thought I was the only one.'

He paused. 'Well, it's a long story. It kinda starts when I was a kid.' He stopped again. 'I'm telling it all wrong. I mean, I can't remember a time when that stuff wasn't going on. Right beside my bed, when I was little, I'd see a man watching over me when I slept. My momma told me he was there to protect me.'

'You've seen things – people?' I couldn't imagine the awfulness of it.

He ducked his head. 'Yeah. I've thought about it a lot and I guess crossing the borders is like climbing rungs on a ladder. First step is feeling things are weird, or a bit wrong. Then comes hearing. Then seeing. I'm at a different level of the ladder than you, because I've seen stuff too. Not just felt it.'

As he talked, I felt a slow sigh of relief escape me. *Not mad*, my mind insisted. *Not mad like the people from the home up the road with their slurred, muffled speech, and their slow, blank eyes. Just sane. Just like Charles.* I felt my old never-voiced terror start to wash out in great, breathless surges.

Charles left Paris soon afterwards. I was only consoled by the thought I would follow him to London to stay in his aunt's apartment. A few weeks later, after a prolonged over-night coach-ride in a bus where the French driver played rap music and no-one slept, I arrived in London with Adele, full of tired elation to see him again.

And it was lovely. The glad, face-aching smiles at meet-ing again, the trip round the supermarket to buy food and strong cider for the evening. Over the bread counter he held my arm. 'I am really so glad you've come over.' I felt a little, warm wriggle of happiness in my stomach. Adele walked back with us, agreeing to stay for dinner before meeting her relatives in Camden. We were all tired, but it felt nice to reassemble part of the old Paris group. In fact everything was lovely until we got back to his aunt's apartment in Battersea. Nice neighbourhood, rows of Sloaney houses and tidy trees. The people were smartly dressed; even the dogs looked more manicured than usual.

Then I stepped in the door of the apartment. It was all wrong. The sunlight of the late afternoon lay flat and yellow against the walls, which seemed just a little darker at the top than they should be. It was quiet and a little cold, despite the golden heat of the summer day outside.

The corridor in front was a pool of empty silence.

I looked around out of the corners of my eyes.

'This is nice.' Adele enthused. Charles looked at me sideways. I opened my mouth to politely agree, and then closed it again.

Rosemary's Baby, went the insistent voice in my head. *It's like the apartment in Rosemary's Baby.*

My mind felt slow and puzzled. No it didn't. There was really no physical resemblance.

'Grocery bags?' Charles was still watching me.

'Oh yes!' Confused, I followed him to the cool, white kitchen and started unpacking.

Later that night, we were tired and a little drunk, especially Adele and Charles. I'd tried to explain that English cider was stronger than French, but their blurred, pink faces told me they hadn't listened. My home-made hamburger lay half-finished on my plate, bleeding ketchup. My mouth was almost too weary to chew.

Yawning and lusting for sleep, I stumbled into the spare bedroom, savouring the smell of fresh cotton and the cool, slithery mass of pillows. I lay half-awake in a sensuous swoon of fatigue. At the end of the corridor I could hear Adele laughing at the door, then sounds of diligent, drunk Charles clearing up in the kitchen, banging plates and glasses heavily against the draining board. And then silence. My eyes closed and I stretched out my throbbing leg muscles.

Seconds later, I was awake, exasperated. Upstairs, there was the distinct sound of feet walking then running, a quick, light thumping. It was no use. The running feet were in my head, real and visible. Round and round they went. My shut eyes projected visions of them, neatly shod in trainers, completing perfect circuits, over and over, overhead.

I'll never sleep now, I thought, almost savage with tiredness. *Stop running!*

And then it was morning. A smell of coffee and toasting bagels drifted into the room. I sniffed. Sesame seeds? My stomach remembered my half-finished dinner and propelled me up.

Charles sat with his back to the window. His hair was unusually unkempt, the back sticking straight up, framing his head like a spiky halo. He snapped the lid of his Zippo back, cigarette tilted between his lips. I took a bagel and buttered it.

'You OK?'

'Yeah, fine, feel a lot better. Except for your bloody neighbour keeping me awake.' I smiled to bely my angry words, last night's annoyance fading.

He looked directly at me.

'Your upstairs neighbour walking round and round. Actually, it was more like a run. Weird time of night for it.'

Charles exhaled, dropped his eyes to stare at the cigarette in his hand. 'There is no upstairs,' he said quietly. 'This is the top apartment.' The bagel felt like dough in my mouth. 'There was no-one upstairs.' He kept his gaze on his hand, tapping the cigarette into the ashtray. 'But you're right. There were a lot walking last night.'

'Who was walking?' My voice was tiny, my insides airless.

'Well, y'all for a start.'

Fear hung low and cold inside me. 'Me?'

'Yes,' he said quietly. 'Found you in the kitchen. Fast asleep. I guess you were sleepwalking. Walking the borderlines.' He ground out his cigarette, hard, and looked up. His blue eyes seemed glassy as marbles. 'But I do think you heard footsteps. That running sounds right.'

'It's this apartment, isn't it?' My voice felt dry and light in my throat. 'There's something wrong here. Tell me what it is!'

'I don't know what it is. But that running sounds right,' he repeated slowly. 'Whatever's here is restless, moving.'

'I knew when I came in. I just didn't know why.'

'I was watching you to see. If you saw...' I heard the same tightness in his voice as I felt in my own. 'Look honey, I've been here for two nights on my own already. I wasn't sure if it was just me.' I moved the chair to sit close to him, craving the solid feel of him, cheek against the fabric of his white T-shirt. My mind marvelled – *Two nights of this! On his own!*

'What *is* it?'

He shrugged, and I felt him breathe in deep under his t-shirt. 'Look, I'll take you round. See if y'all can feel anything.'

Small steps. We walked slowly from the front door, down the corridor. Into the kitchen. Fine. The living room was a little chilly, a little dark. The bathroom was gray and dull. For a second, a shadow chased past the corner of my eye. My heartbeat jackhammered. I couldn't drag my gaze to the mirror beside the sink.

Charles held my arm. 'No, not there,' I said, flatly.

We walked into the master bedroom, Charles's room. There was nothing there. Except at the top of the walls.

Twenty minutes later, we were standing outside the front door, not speaking. We were holding hands like children, gripping each other, tugging downwards. Our rucksacks spilled clothes at our feet.

What did we see in that room? My mind has rolled over that memory so many times that it is as flat and unrealistic as a poor effect in an old B-movie. It was a movement, darkness, a shadow, nothing more. But as I looked at it, it seemed to stretch and grow, to pulse with an oily black shimmer.

It's not even a dramatic story, is it? In the end, all I saw were shadows. What I didn't realise back then was that shadows are everywhere. When you cross a border, things are never quite the same. Now I see the darkness everywhere. It follows me, stealthy as a black cat. I see it sometimes, half-glimpsed, on the edges of vision. Sometimes I think I see it behind my eyes at night. That's what I fear most. Whatever lies beyond our borders moves easiest in the darkness. All borderliners know that.

Charles and I didn't really stay in touch. Sometimes experience draws you closer together. Sometimes it has the opposite effect. I think that privately we were reluctant to be near each other, in case our combined presence attracted anything else. He did come to see me in Dublin, towards the end of his backpacking year. It wasn't a great success, with little time to talk. Besides, things that seemed interesting or philosophical in Paris and urgently important in London just felt odd and off-kilter against the normality of home. Afterwards we wrote to each other in a haphazard fashion. He moved to Canada, fell in love with a lawyer. I heard he was engaged to her and I wrote to congratulate him.

It was just yesterday that I heard about it in an e-mail from Adele. She must have stayed in touch with him. '*Isn't it so sad about Charles? What a lovely guy. I can't believe he's gone.*

I'm sitting on the seat in my back garden, thinking about him. It's a crisp autumn evening, and the lawn looks like dark, soft velvet in the twilight. His twenty year old self is so clear in my mind, even though almost everything he said to me and I to him is lost, when he is just a smile in a photo album, when I don't even have his address anymore. I recall that eye-meet in the hostel lobby, that clicking into sharp focus, that whirling sense of recognition, that inevitability of speech. If I weaken and remember the whole story, I will move the darkness closer to me. I concentrate on trying to retain that memory of sunshine and eager chat, his smiling face, his southern drawl. I'm making an image to hold on to like a talisman, to sustain me through the long night ahead.

Yet, in spite of my best efforts, I can't stop it. My fists unclench, I give way. I remember our journey to the borders, the pulsing blackness that we found there. As I sit in the dusk, cold tears edge down my face, tears for Charles who tried to outrun the shadows and failed, Charles who spent so many years walking the borderlines, Charles who has left me alone in the darkness.

LONG SHADOWS

I fidget in the waiting room like I always do, in every waiting room I've ever been in. My mouth seems too full, of teeth, of tongue, of saliva. I shift in my seat and feel my heart beat like a quickened metronome. According to the loudly ticking clock on the wall, I've been here for five minutes. Five minutes of flipping disdainfully through the limp magazines on the table – *Really? Last summer's Vogue?* – and flicking the rejected ones onto a pile of discards. I look at the clock. Six minutes. Then seven. The second hand ticks by deliberately. I feel a tight, wrathful feeling start to bubble in the pit of my stomach. I have no talent for waiting.

'Ms. Scorton?' The receptionist has returned. She is brisk and dainty, hair coiffed neatly as an air hostess. 'Doctor Smith is ready for you now.' I follow her demure kitten heels across a padded carpet. She pauses and gives me a bright, insincere smile as she opens the door to his office.

'So. Dreams.' He nods his head and pushes his fleshy lips together into a judicious pucker. 'Hmm.' He is much as I remember, but his thick hair is greying, and he is wearing thick-framed glasses. He writes something down on the expensive-looking leather book of creamy paper opened in front of him. 'And they are upsetting you, these dreams?'

I nod.

'Yes. They keep coming, night after night. Again and again. It's gotten to the point where I don't want to sleep – where I'm *afraid* to sleep.' I hear the tell-tale waver in my voice and stop, clamping my lips together in a hard line. I am desperate to stop myself from melting into a low wail, from giving in to the hoarse, bawling sobs that are brewing up inside me. His face, so familiar to me, is creased and soft with pity.

'Sophie,' he says. 'Don't hold it in. Tell me all about it. I'm here to help.' I can only nod helplessly. Inside a piercing train whistle of grief is building up. I don't dare open my lips to release it, or I won't be able to stop. I think he senses this, because he looks away, tactfully, at his wall of gilt-framed certificates to give me time to master my tidal wave of self-pity. And I do.

'Yes.' I say finally, tightly, and give a small, quick nod. He looks at me, then again, carefully.

'Is it the fact that I've known you and your family for years, Sophie? Do you think this would be better with someone else? Perhaps a woman? Someone more your age? I won't be offended, I promise you.' His voice is measured, low, comforting. 'I can write you a referral, if you want?'

'It's fine.' My voice is barely a whisper. Inside I finish the sentence, meanly adding *because you won't charge me for this session.* Instead I say aloud, 'I don't mind. I kind of find it reassuring. To be honest I need some reassur–' My sentence ends in a rough sob. I stop and raise my knuckles to my mouth. He lets my silence grow for one, two, three beats, then cuts back in.

'Why don't you tell me about these dreams?'

I sit up straighter in the chair. 'OK.' I lower my hand back into my lap, and begin. 'So the dreams are often different, different scenarios, but they all have something in common. They all have *him* in common. It's…' I stop again, confused.

He is nodding now. 'Take it slowly. Begin at the beginning.' I lower my head, inhale and then exhale, one long, deep breath that makes me feel slightly dizzy. Then I begin again.

'So. The first dream. I guess you want them in order?'

He nods. 'That would be helpful, yes.'

'Right.' Another deep breath. 'I dreamt I was at the beach. The same beach we used to go to when I was a child. It was a beautiful day.' I remember the dream. It felt so real. I could sense the warmth of the sun on my arms. I could smell the unique salt-sand-drains stink of the seaside, and hear the shrieks of the gulls mingle with the shouts of children and the gusty blasts of music from the amusements. I shake myself out of my reverie. 'Anyway, the beach was full of people, and noisy, but over all the commotion I heard the tinkly little tune of an ice-cream van.' I swallow. 'It was playing Yankee Doodle Dandy. I looked and saw it down at the end of the beach, all bright colours and pictures of ice-cream cones. It started to drive slowly down the beach towards me, and it was then I noticed that it was simply rolling over the bodies of the sunbathers. On and on it came, and as it came closer, I could hear faint cries and screams, as though the people were in a bell-jar, with almost no sound escaping. As the wheel touched each person they would dissolve into heaps of dry, brown leaves. And all the time...' I pause and take a drink from the red glass tumbler in front of me. *No plastic cups here*, I think sardonically. It tastes tinny and unpleasant. 'And all the time it kept playing Yankee Doodle Dandy. Finally the van ground to a stop beside me. I looked inside the open window, and there he was, grinning.' I pause and shiver – a quick shudder of recollection. 'He leaned out of the van. "I'm coming," he said, and smiled even more widely. "I'm coming for you." From behind him a torrent of dry leaves started to spill out of the van, great gouts of decaying leaves. They kept hitting my face, clinging to my hair, my clothes. I was trying to brush them off, faster and faster. When I woke up, I was screaming.'

'Fascinating.' He puts down his silver pen carefully. There are a lot of unintelligible marks on the cream paper before him. 'So who is this man?'

I shake my head in frustration. 'I don't *know*.' I blurt out, frustrated. 'I just have the feeling I've seen him before, somewhere. It's the smile. I know I recognise it.'

'But you don't recognise him?' I shake my head again.

'But he makes me feel angry,' I supply. 'And scared. I asked my parents if I ever had a fright at the seaside as a child.'

'And had you?'

I wave a hand in dismissal. 'Not a sausage. No drownings or accidents witnessed. No flashers. No momentous occasions, not even getting lost.'

'I remember you then,' he says. 'At the beach. You and your sister, like little golden-haired angels.' His voice is gentle. I remember us too, fearless and laughing and endlessly confident.

'Yes,' I say, wryly. 'I was pretty happy then.'

He gives me a close look. 'And now?'

I shrug. 'Dunno. I feel sometimes that nothing's kind of lived up to what I thought it would be. You know, being a grown-up, moving out. It's the Celtic Tiger backlash, isn't it?

No jobs, no houses.' He is writing again, but still looking me in the eye. They must learn that kind of multitasking at medical college.

'This disturbs you? Do you have a job?'

'What Douglas Coupland would call a McJob.' I like to drop in the literary reference to show that I am not completely brain-dead. 'I work in a coffee shop in the city. I make coffee and clear tables. It's OK. I dropped out of college.' I add, though I am sure my parents have told him. 'Without a degree I don't have a huge lot of options. A friend of mine has a PhD and she hasn't even had an interview in a year.'

'And now you are having these upsetting dreams?'

'Are you asking if they're linked to my nowhere-job?'

His face is neutral. 'Are you telling me they are?'

I shake my head crossly. 'No. I think they're about something else.'

'Very well.' He puts down his pen again. 'And this dream has recurred?'

'Yes,' I say. 'Would you like me to tell you about the next time?'

'Please.' So I do.

'OK, the second dream was set in my primary school. A strange location – I don't think I've given it a thought since I left it. In the dream I was the age I am now, but I was also in class, I don't know, maybe fourth or fifth class? All around me I could see familiar-looking people – a girl from my apartment building, the man who runs the grocery store beside my café – and we're all being tested on our spellings. Spelling tests used to freak me out when I was a kid; I would study and study the prescribed words, and worry so much about getting one wrong. I feel exactly the same here. I'm starting to panic as the teacher is pointing at people closer and closer to me. I'm spelling their words to myself and I keep getting them wrong.' I wince at the sharp memory of panic, feeling the words jumble and slur in my head. 'Just as it comes to my turn, the classroom door opens. It's the same man from my earlier dream, still smiling. His teeth are big and white, too big for his face. "I'm coming to get you," he says with a big, wolfish smile. I look at the teacher, alarmed, but I see her nodding. She is letting him take me away. Part of me is relieved about escaping the spelling test, but a bigger part of me is afraid of him. He walks over to my desk. "Come on," he says softly. All I can see are his great big teeth framing the great big hole of his mouth. I feel myself start to tip over. I'm falling, falling down, down, down, inside his huge mouth. When I wake up, I'm on the floor. Crying. My heart's beating really quickly, so quickly it hurts my chest.'

He is writing now, faster and faster. I clasp my hands between my legs and wait. Eventually he looks up. 'Is that it?'

'That's it for that one. But there've been more dreams. Most I don't remember as vividly. But I see him in familiar locations like my old house, my back yard. Sometimes I just dream that I see him on the street, an innocuous passerby. Innocuous, that is, until I see his smile. And in every dream he tells me he is coming back, coming to get me.'

'And these dreams have just started? Have you had them before?'

'Not for a long, long time.' I dimly remember some childhood nightmares, rich and baroque, waiting by my parents' bed, begging them to let me in. 'To be honest the last time I remember having dreams like that is when I was a kid.'

'And were they similar dreams?' I pause, and think, trying to recapture my childhood dreams, as elusive as a forgotten scent, or the sound of a long-ago voice.

'There was one about a giant, I remember,' I say doubtfully. I close my eyes and try to visualise it. It slides out of my memory with surprising ease. 'In the dream he was always running after me, relentlessly, chasing me around the house. I would try and hide, but each time the hiding place would be too small, part of me would be sticking out, an arm, a leg. Then he would see me, and the chase would be on again. I would finally wake when he reached out and grabbed me.'

'So this is the last set of recurring dreams that you remember before the onset of the current ones?'

'I think so,' I say uncertainly. 'To be honest, I don't remember a lot of my adult dreams, just the odd one. But these are different. Technicolour. Full sound. Like being in a horror film.'

'There is a lot of anxiety here, alright,' he says, almost to himself. 'So these are the only dreams you remember clearly?'

'Not quite.' My voice is almost steady. 'I had another one last night.' I lift the tumbler from the desk and set it down precisely. 'This time when I had the dream, I wasn't even sure it *was* a dream. I mean, I was lying in bed, but at the same time dreaming I was lying in bed in my old home. It was a summer night, and I was restless with heat. Every time I tried to roll over, the duvet and sheets would catch me up, and wind more tightly round me, so I was in a cocoon. It was a very realistic dream. I imagined I could feel sweat dampening my back, and prickling my forehead, waves of heat breaking up and down me. Then I heard it. A knock. In the dream, I woke up, and sat up in bed. The sound came again, but this time it wasn't a single knock, but a series of light taps. Now, I'm not a fan of the dark. When I was a child, I always needed to sleep with a nightlight.'

He nods, remembering, or at least pretending to.

'So in the dream – I know I keep repeating that, but that's because it felt like I was really awake all this time – I switched on the bedside lamp. There was nothing there.' My voice falters. 'Sorry. I feel a bit wobbly, talking about this.'

He is soothing. 'Don't worry, you're doing just fine. Just keep going, if you can. Everything you tell me about these dreams is helpful.' I rub my hands, suddenly sweaty, on the sides of the chair.

'So I listen again, intently. I can feel my heart banging in my eardrums. Then I hear that light knocking again, with absolute clarity. I grab my pillow and hug it to my face. I am very frightened. Through half-closed eyes I see the wardrobe door, just in range of my peripheral vision, start to swing outwards. I am awash with terror. My body, so hot a moment ago, is goose-pimpled with ice. The door is still slowly opening, and to my rising horror, I see there is a shape inside the wardrobe. He steps out, still shadowed by the wardrobe. His mouth and hands are full of dead leaves that he drops on the floor. I can see his terrible smile, all teeth. "I'm coming," he says, leaning over me. "I'm almost here." There are leaves falling from his mouth onto my face. I open my mouth to scream and I feel it fill with their gelid dampness. When I wake up, I'm doing this awful airless scream, no sound, just a terrified wheeze. I can barely breathe.' I stop. My hands are shaking. I shove them up my sleeves.

There is a silence. 'I can't keep doing this,' I say. 'I'm afraid to sleep. And then I still have to work, so I drink coffee to keep me awake, and that gives me palpitations. Then I can't sleep, and when I do I wake in a panic.'

He nods. 'Sophie, it sounds to me like you are suffering from panic attacks that seem to manifest largely in your dreams. Do you feel like you normally express anxieties to others?'

I think about it. 'Not really. Well, I try not to think too much about stuff. Life. Big things. I like being shallow. I think about going to gigs and men and TV.' I tip my head to one side, defiantly. 'I'm not one of those bores who drone on about themselves. I'm fine. The only reason I came here is that the dreams are interfering with my life. They're bothering me.'

'So–' He reads from his notes '–would it be fair to say that you don't like to think over-much about matters that actively bother you?' I nod. 'And you prefer to repress these thoughts rather than let them surface?' I nod again. He looks at me thoughtfully. ''Where do you think these thoughts go? These negative thoughts you don't allow yourself to have?'

I am surprised by the question. 'I don't know. I've never thought about that.'

'Well, I can tell you that these thoughts, these emotions don't just disappear over time. They tend to resurface, sometime in unexpected times, in unexpected places, and can emerge as panic attacks. Your mention–' he refers to his notes again '–of breathlessness, chest pains, tears, feelings of vertigo, all correspond to this. The good news is, we can work on this. There are several excellent anti-anxiety drugs we can try.'

I look up. 'Will it stop the dreams?'

He nods. 'In time. I'll also advise you to come back for a few sessions. It would be important to keep following up on your treatment with a series of relaxation exercises, in order to control your anxieties before sleeping.' I barely hear him. Inside me, the relief is surging up. *No more dreams*, I think, *no more night terrors.*

He sees me to the door. 'Take care of yourself, won't you Sophie? I hope that this has helped.'

'It feels like it has,' I say gratefully. 'Thank you.' He motions away my attempts to pay him. I see his secretary's perfect eyebrows arch in surprise at his generosity. 'No, Sophie. This is for old times' sake. But come again. Come back again.' He smiles, his eyes crinkling in a maze of friendly creases.

I step out into the street. Leaves blow in drifts down the footpath, brown and rustling. I pause. Those words. That *smile.* I am electrified by a sudden, strange image. *Can it be?*

I step back inside. 'Doctor Smith?' I say uncertainly. The reception is dark. Someone has switched off the main lamp. The desk is deserted. 'Doctor Smith?' I call, louder this time. 'I've remembered something.' The doorknob of his office turns smoothly in my hand.

'Doctor?' He is standing at the window, with his back turned to me. 'Doctor,' I say. 'I think he's coming.'

He turns and smiles – that *smile.*

'No,' he says. 'He's here.'

THE WOMAN NEXT DOOR

I'm tired all the time since he came. Tired and overwhelmed and overpowered by the feelings, the smells, the sounds, the weight and feel of him. He was part of my body, sleeping tight under my skin. Now he's out, we're apart yet never-apart, all at once. His warm, soft scent, the silken fluff of his head, the tiny perfection of his feet, all these fill my senses; they intoxicate me. I love him. I resent him. He's the biggest thing that's ever happened to me. He's everything, all the time. My body is still connected to his through a complex and invisible set of nerve endings. His cat-cries wake me, alert, from sleep. Sometimes I see Sean, a lump of sleep beside me, and my foggy brain thinks it might hate him if I ever had the time or energy to do so.

It's only been three weeks and my home has been invaded. Its new, tiny overlord has possessions strewn every-where. Clothes horses are filled with drying baby-grows, there are a pile of presents at the foot of the stairs that I'll take up someday when I remember. It's horrifying. In the minutes here and there, when I come out of my baby-haze of sleepwalking through life in odd socks, I see my home, layered in dust, piles of laundry in the kitchen and smeared surfaces everywhere. Part of me knows this is just a phase, but the rest of me is just quietly appalled by my own descent. Sometimes I catch sight of my face flashing up in a mirror, a glass pane, startled, pale, haunted, and I wonder – *is this me?* Can this really be the me I remember from a scant few months ago? That woman in heels, hair pulled back smartly in a shining chignon, Kate Spade handbag in one hand, mobile phone in the other? I can see her, as if through a mist, but I no longer believe I *was* her. My hair is always knotted now; it's been in the same ragged ponytail for days. Yesterday I dropped my mobile in the baby bath, and my glossy handbag has been replaced by a pouchy, plastic ham-mock from M&S, stuffed with nappies and bottles. My body hurts, stiff and sore, so I swathe it carefully in layers of soft, brushed cotton, worn trackpants, fluffy bedsocks, any-thing large and comforting to wear. My belly still juts out, embarrassingly so, as if he's still in there. I love him, but this is what he's done to me. He has taken me over.

The woman next door isn't like that. I can't stop watching her. She's our new neighbour, moved in when I was in hospital. She is everything that I want to be. As I sit up at night, rocking him to sleep; that ancient, aging ritual of soothing a mewling child, I see her come home, her heels tap-tapping smartly on the pavement, her long blonde hair swaying behind her, glinting under the streetlights. She's glossy and pretty in a carefully-manicured way. (I bet she has a *great* manicure too). Her clothes are a symphony of creams and caramels, swingy camel capes, belted French trench-coats, tissue-soft brown leather jackets. I imagine their smell, warm and fragrant like a subtle floral perfume. Her figure is elegant; she strides confidently about in knee-high boots, her concave thighs inspiring a soft, sad kind of lust in me. On the days when the baby cries unstoppably, when the noise fills my head till I think I might scream too, I want to be her so badly, I half-wonder if I can simply will it to happen.

Sean can't understand my fascination with her.

'She's only a woman, for God's sake,' he says dismissively. We are having a miserable meal, microwaved rice and chicken in a sauce from a jar. It says tikka masala on the label, but it's rust-brown and smells faintly of gas. I just know that next door, the woman is laying down heavy, silver cutlery on dense, white napkins, lighting candles and bringing food carefully out of the oven – a herbed omelette, perhaps, or a perfect chocolate soufflé? I push away my plate of lukewarm rice mush. Sean is eating away steadily, his hair rumpled from his long commute home on the train. He looks tired too, but I have no pity. He goes away every weekday to a place with coffee that other people make. He talks to grownups for pleasure, about the weather, TV, sports. People invite him for lunch... A thin, seagull cry blurts from the baby monitor. I'm already on my feet, moving instinctively upstairs. My legs are leaden, like when you get out of weightless water after swimming. When I get to the cot, he's back asleep, his fat little body gloriously splayed, his face twisted in a majestic, thunderous frown. I love him. I hate him.

I sit beside him and look out the window into the neighbouring backyard. A soft pool of light gleams in it, illuminating her neatly cut grass, her trimmed hedges. She's sitting out there, on one of her cast-iron chairs, her legs neatly crossed. There's a glass in front of her and a book. I feel my insides twist with envy. I remember all those days I sat carelessly half-reading, flicking through pages, those marvellously blank, indolent days of pregnancy; how I took that idleness for granted. Now I'm a perpetual-motion mummy-machine, picking up, wiping, soothing and feeding. I touch my fingers to the pane, lightly. She tilts her head to one side and looks directly up at me. I jump back from the window as if it has shocked me, ashamed, embarrassed to be caught staring like an envious wraith from a darkened window.

'Laura!' It's Sean, I remember. These days I forget him as soon as he leaves the room. I run down the stairs silently, angrily.

'Don't shout!' I hiss. 'Don't wake him.'

Sean looks abashed. 'Sorry,' he says contritely. 'Can I go up and see Jack?' I sit down. It's still strange to me that he has a name. In my head he is just Him, all powerful, almighty Him.

'Sure,' I say listlessly. 'But don't wake him. I need some time. I need to do–' I wave a limp hand at the congealed dishes, the dirty table, the spattered wads of kitchen roll '– this.' He nods and disappears upstairs. I pick up the plates and put them in the sink, then just stand there, dull and unmoving, hands on the sticky draining board. He's too much. It's too much. I can't do it. No one told me it would be so incessant. I am not me anymore. I am a corpulent mummy-monster, performing endless placatory rituals to assuage a screaming, soaking god. I sigh, a deep, juddering sigh, then hunker down and open the fridge to start preparing bottles for the night feeds. I hear the monitor crackle, then there's a hiccup, a choke and a wail. I close my eyes, feeling the light of the refrigerator dance pink behind my eyelids. I put the bottles back, as delicately as the anger in me will allow.

#

It's morning. I watch her from the kitchen window. She comes out in that smart cape with the three sparkling buttons at the neck, leather satchel over one shoulder, carrying a pink baby-seat. Yes. I haven't told you about that. It's the worst bit. She has a baby too. She has a baby and she looks terrific. Her body is slim and elegant; her clothes are carefully chosen and co-ordinated. Her baby girl never seems to scream; I can see her face quarter-turned away as she gently places the baby-seat in the back of the car. Every day she drops her off and goes to work, that magic place where no one soils themselves, or spits up milk, or cries for hours, endlessly, mysteriously. She is everything I am not. Quick, she's seen me. She turns on one heel and waves at me brightly, before stepping into her car. I stand there, lumpish, tired, my hair itching with grease, my skin grey and dry as sandpaper and I cry fat, silent, oozing tears. I feel full of sadness, swollen with misery, as if the slightest bend or tilt might unleash waves of tears from over the barricades of my eyelids.

I don't even know her name. I pretend it is something exotic: Anais, Veronique, Isolda. In my imagination she runs a magazine or a model agency. She drinks skinny cappuccinos and goes shopping for shoes at lunchtime.

Sean is getting increasingly annoyed by my obsession. 'How much time do you spend mooning over her? Couldn't you just introduce yourself?'

I can't explain why not, why her very presence fills me with shame for my weakness, my bulk, my secret tears.

'I'm sure she's grand,' he continues. 'I sometimes see her on the train and she looks friendly. She's said hello once or twice. Go on, why don't you make friends? Her baby would be company for Jack when he's older. Besides, she's probably lonely.'

I don't think she's lonely even though I've never seen anyone else visit the house. I think she's self-contained, precise and perfect in her pristine glass bubble of a life. Sean has no idea what she means to me. I look at him eating tonight's culinary disaster (pork chops and potato – no vegetables and no sauce) and feel a gush of hot hatred for his solid, chewing head.

#

Days go by. I wish I could say I get used to it all. But I don't. Instead I stumble in a grey fog, vision blurred with tiredness but guided by a series of bat-squeaks and howls, as I try to calculate what's needed, what's happening, what's hurting. Sometimes when I arrive at the cot his eyes squint crossly at me, like the middle manager of a supermarket upbraiding the checkout staff. I want to cry and apologise. Once I fell asleep hanging over his cot; when I woke up he was staring at me, affronted, face contorted in a dreadful infant rage.

Somehow I blunder through it, the dull days of crying and laundry, the nights of pacing and rocking. Sean is out there somewhere in the ether, a shadowy presence, whose life intersects with mine in the evenings. We've established a new mode of being; a badly-cooked meal in return for stories from the outside world. We're slipping away from each other, fast and silent, as the days go by. I remember being in love with him, but distantly. It seems like a poor, weak thing compared to this compulsive baby-need that surrounds me. We're more of a team now: me chief nurse, him a disinterested supervisor. But I try. I cook quick, hopeless meals – beans on toast, pasta and readymade tomato sauce, canned chili. And he talks about Veda.

See? I was right. Her name *was* exotic. He's struck up a few chats with her and every evening I question him like a detective. She is (he thinks) in her mid-thirties. She doesn't seem to have a boyfriend. She runs a travel agency, so instead of picturing her flicking frosty glances over starved model bodies, I visualise her spinning a globe with one painted fingernail as she talks to a client. She has a baby girl. He thinks she is called Kate or Katie. I feel a stab of envy that she can choose to discuss her child or not; that she neatly divorces woman from mother every morning when she steps on that train. Sean asks me if we should invite her over. I demur. He shrugs. I don't tell him my pathetic fantasy of looking better and losing weight before we meet. This fantasy gets more hopeless by the day as I stand over the sink eating buttered toast with jam in fast, shameful, secret bites.

One day I do bump into her. He's been crying all day so I manhandle him into the pram, the stiff starfish shape of him rigid in protest, and strap him in. 'We'll see if being outside helps,' I tell him desperately. I trundle the pram across the gravelled drive which bumps him and makes him crosser. At the gate I pause to open it when – oh no! It's her! At her gate! I can't escape.

'Hello,' I say miserably. I drop my gaze and see myself with a shock of revulsion; a stained tracksuit, a pair of Sean's socks, dirty Crocs.

'Hello there,' she whispers back. She's carrying her perfect daughter in a neat baby sling. She puts a finger to her lips. 'Sleeping,' she breathes, and I nod, relieved to have an excuse not to talk. From the pram comes a low, choking wail. I look at him, sticky face, open, gummy mouth and feel an absurd desire to grab her sleeping child and run off, leaving my yowling one behind. Of course I don't. I smile, bob my head quickly in a meaningless gesture, and push the pram through the gate.

'So you finally met Veda?' asks Sean that evening, settling down his worn leather man-bag. *I should get him a new one* I think, and then automatically add it to the never-ending list of things to get, like underwear that fits me, cleaning spray, a new lawnmower. 'She was delighted to finally meet you; she even said she might call over. I told her this evening would be fine.' He looks at me expectantly.

I am startled. 'What? I can't do this evening. It's my new fitness class!' He looks blank, as well he might. I've just made it up, but am banking on his bad memory. 'But it would be nice for you,' he coaxes. I look around wildly at the chaos, our life, me, and I know I can't have it examined by the perfect woman next door.

I have to leave for my imaginary class, so I drive around aimlessly until I see a coffee-shop open. I order a sweet, rich mocha and sip it till the heat and the sugar warms me up. For an hour, a whole glorious hour, I watch people go by, chat, drink coffee. I read a newspaper someone has left behind and eat a cranberry oat cookie. It is heavenly. For the first time in almost two months I feel myself relax, feel that I can do this strange and complex thing called motherhood. I just need a break; to remember that the world of restaurants, hotels and magazines still exists out there.

When I come home the house is peaceful. Sean is watching TV, the dishwasher is thrumming away gently and the landfill of clutter seems to have receded. I sling my gym bag over the chair and breathe in deeply.

'Is he..?'

'Asleep,' confirms Sean. 'Pity you missed Veda. She got a babysitter in and everything. And she was great with Jack. She had him off in minutes – sang to him. She even gave me a hand with the tidying.'

My stomach sinks; there's a red knot of shame in my throat. 'Oh,' I say, faintly. Sean gets up and hugs me. 'And it's so good for you to get out more. Veda says it's important.' I lie into his hug, trying to forget the embarrassment of another woman cleaning up my filthy home. He kisses my hair, beside my ear. 'Tell you what,' he says thickly, into my hair. 'Tomorrow's Saturday. Take a few hours off in the morning. Treat yourself.'

And I do. The next morning I leave without the heavy buggy or the car-seat. A miracle of unimpeded motion. I go to a big, cheap high-street store and buy some smart ankle boots, a long, soft cardigan, a cheap but colourful necklace, and a forgiving, pretty smocked top. I go into the public toilets and change out of my old tracksuit and trainers and stuff them in a bin. I'll probably regret this when I get home, but I can't bear to keep them now. I have my hair cut and blow-dried. I don't care that the junior washing my hair is appalled by its state.

'It's awfully tangled,' she says dubiously. 'I'll have to cut it up a bit.' When I come out, hair bobbed neatly and smelling of some mysterious, fruity product, I feel transformed.

'Look at you!' Sean's approval shines out at me. He takes my arm and rotates me, carefully, as if he held me too hard, this shiny new vision might crack and unleash my old tattered self.

'Thank you.' I say softly. 'Thank you for remembering me.' He smiles, that old, warm smile that always makes my mouth curl upwards in response.

'That's not all,' he says. 'Look!'

I see two suitcases in the hall. *Is he going? Am I?* – I turn, momentarily terrified.

'It's a *treat*,' he says, half-laughing at my surprise. 'We're off to that nice B&B we went to for Claire's wedding. Just us.'

My heart is beating blood through my ears in a long, drowning roar.

'Where is he?'

'Jack's fine,' says Sean confidently. 'Veda has him. She offered. We've been planning this for you for a while. I knew you needed a break.' He pauses and smiles at me. 'She just helped me with the final details.'

I am weak, dizzy. 'You gave him to her?' My voice is coming from somewhere outside me, weak and breathy. Everything inside me is focusing on staying upright.

'Yeah. He's over there right now...Wait! Are you OK?' His voice is alarmed. I look at him and start running. I pelt down the garden path, one of my stupid new boots I was so proud of buckles under me and throws me to the ground. I land, palms flat on the gravel that bites into my flesh like knives. I register the pain somewhere at the back of my mind, but I keep running, then I'm there, pounding on her door.

'Where is he?' I shout. Sean is behind me, grabbing my wrists.

'Shhh!' he says hoarsely. 'Stop it!' A woman on the road has paused to watch, two children have stopped cycling to stare instead. I don't care.

'Let me in!' I'm ringing the doorbell frantically between repeated knocks. There's no answer. Sean is calling my name, urgently, over and over. I can't look at him. *I was in the hairdressers!* I think wildly. *I was buying clothes!* Instantly I need him, I need his warm heft in my arms, his milky breath against my neck. My baby; the most solid, true and beautiful miracle of my life. I've started crying now, deep, grating sobs. No-one's answering the door. I'm beyond caring what I do. I pick up a smooth, spherical stone from her rockery and lob it through the thick glass pane on the front door. My hand scrapes through and opens the lock. It comes out red and wet. Sean tries to grab it.

'Jesus! What've you done!' But I'm off, inside, running.

'Where are you?' I run, crying, heels clattering through an immaculate kitchen, then a bare sitting room. I'm terrified, cold, stone terrified. I run upstairs, tripping as I go, then into a bedroom. It's show-home neat. Nothing.

Nobody.

'Laura!' calls Sean. He stands in the doorway of her bedroom. 'She must be here. Her baby's still in the cot.' His face is stunned with relief.

There's a pink, ruffled cot by the window. I whirl around and stand over it. My vision comes and goes in one big, sick blur. I open my mouth, but only a wet, animal sound comes out. In that one, awful moment, I realise it all, the perfection of her home, her limpid, graceful lifestyle. I think wildly of my baby, of his soft starfish fingers pulsing towards me, his hiccupping cry, the warm weight of him on my lap. I open my mouth and finally I name all those things, those smells, sounds, sights, my feelings. 'Jack,' I say softly.

But it's not Jack. What looks back at me, waxen and lifeless, is a doll.

TRACING THE SPECTRE

Afterwards it's hard to recall the exact sequence of events. Some stand out, light-bright, like what happened on the stairs. Others recede into shadows, so that they're confusing to remember. And some of them can never be forgotten.

But I'm beginning in the wrong place. Let me get it in order. I'll tell you about the drive there.

It is a cold drive down through the flat Midlands. The sky glows a sullen dirty grey through the rain-blotched windshield. Ahead are vistas of spiky, mud-coloured trees, their branches hacked into uniform length. The screech-squeak of wipers sliding on the greasy windscreen is rhythmic, atonal, endlessly annoying. All conversation has stopped miles of muddy road ago, the passengers subdued and quiet as the chill of mid-morning subsides into the warm fug of crowded bodies. In the front, the annoying Californian woman Skye is fidgeting irritably with the radio dials. She's already insisted on sitting in front – 'If I don't I get real nauseous' – and complained bitterly about the quality of the airport coffee. I could tell her the radio doesn't actually work, but a mean part of me lets her continue to fiddle with it. She gives up eventually, after producing only static. I keep steering the car down the wet roads, eyes aching from the queer unrelenting brightness of the sky.

And still the rain continues, driving, relentless.

A dirty rain spatters like snow on the windshield. Whirls of water spray ahead, ricocheting off the road to form a solid layer of mist. It has been a sludgy crawl through wet, grey, low-set towns with their abandoned roadworks, great pools of water stippled with raindrops in torn-up tarmacadam. Though the streets are thronged with parked cars, the towns are curiously lifeless, with only the odd lone, hunched figure hurrying through the spitting rain. Inside, the windows slowly cover with condensation, reducing the visibility even further. And so it goes on, town after town, field after field, wall after wall, until finally, in the late afternoon, the car swings in between the tall grey pillars that stand at the end of the muddy drive of Knocknamara Castle.

'Man. That's some driveway.' Bill, the laconic guy from Texas has woken up. He peers forward, head almost on my shoulder. We bump down the rutted lane with a series of body-jarring jolts.

'Ow,' complains Skye, her face drawn into a frown. 'Watch how you're going!' I say nothing. *Why didn't you offer to drive?* I think savagely, swiping at the condensation on the windscreen. But even I relax when Knocknamara itself comes into view, outlined sharply against the dull white-grey sky. It is a great, vertical mass, built solidly of dark stone, its mock-battlements and decorated pinnacles creating a spectacular Gothic silhouette. Bill emits a low whistle, Skye cranes her neck forward to take it all in, and even quiet English Mark is moved to murmur appreciatively. I pull up in a crunching swirl of gravel and stop. The vast wooden door swings slowly open and I see a woman there, waving at us.

We have arrived.

The caretaker, Mary, leads us in. The entrance hall is impossibly grand, with an immense double staircase rearing up before us. I gently touch the dark, carved wood of the newel post. Mary shows us the library, the grand saloon with its large, pointed windows and glorious fan vaulting, and pauses as we descend the staircase again. 'Now I recommend you stick to the areas I've shown you. You can't go up on the second floor – that's the family's private quarters.' We nod obediently. 'There's no light on the staircase above the second floor, and the third floor has a lot of issues with the roof.' Mark is making notes. Bill, I notice, is shivering visibly. The endless cold of the house is a constant unpleasant surprise, tipping my nose with ice, numbing my toes and breathing blasts of chill air at my face. Skye shivers ostentatiously, despite being wrapped in what seemed to be a belted sleeping-bag. Her raw-boned, red-nosed face peers around, sourly. 'Goddamn it, that curator said this place would be HEATED!' Her voice echoes against the tall walls. 'Well, the kitchen is down here; it's the only warm part of the house at night,' says Mary, ignoring her rudeness and pointing to the left of the staircase. 'We'll light a fire upstairs too, but the ceiling's too high for you to really feel it.'

'Thanks,' I say, as no-one else seems about to. 'Is it OK if we bring in our equipment and set up? Did you say you were lighting a fire in the library?'

'Oh yes. I'll call Jane up to start the fire. I'll be in the kitchen for the next while, but after that she'll be available to you if you need her. She's sleeping here tonight. Well now, in case I don't see you later, good luck to you all.' She scowls briefly at Skye (who is obviously left out of the good wishes) and shakes my hand with a vigorous warmth. She joins the men who are already making their way out to the car, calling to each other across the hallway. Skye digs her hands into her pockets and rocks gently on her heels. 'Let the fun begin,' she says lightly.

We are, as our arts grant application says, *an interdisciplinary team of international artists collaborating on a twenty-four hour project based on artist-led paranormal investigations in Ireland and the US.* It's the second part of the project; the first has already taken place in Tennessee earlier in the year. The project is not my idea – I got drafted in at the last moment, when Carol the Irish photographer decided that being eight months pregnant and spending the night in a dark, haunted castle would be mutually exclusive. So here I am. My job is simple. I am to set up static cameras on timers around the castle – here, in the entrance hall – I put down the camera and carefully check that it is functioning properly – here, in the library – I gently put down my second one. There are two more. *One on the staircase*, I think, *the other in the ballroom?* Finally, with my trusty Nikon, I'll be patrolling at night, at irregular intervals to capture images of transition, from light to darkness. I sit on one of the cold, lumpy chairs in the library and congratulate myself on my solo part in this team project. Nothing to do with the others, thank goodness. I watch them, as they come up the stairs talking. Skye is just a pain in the ass, a born complainer. She is a performance artist – *of course she is*, I think resignedly, who is going to perform a series of interactions with the castle that Mark will film. Mark is OK, I concede, he's just very serious and a little off-putting. I watch his ungainly bespectacled frame as he drags equipment up the stairs. Bill helps him. I have warmed to Bill most of all, partly because of his marvellous Southern twang, but also partly because he has not annoyed me yet. Granted, he slept all of the way here, but he has a drowsy, benign air about him that bodes well. He is a sound artist, he told us, yawning, at the airport. Like me, he is opting for the stealth approach – he wants to set up equipment to monitor and capture different sounds around the castle. In fact the whole project is his idea – a tying together of witch legends from Ireland and Alabama. Outside, the sky looks particularly Irish, a blanket of rough grey hemmed on the horizon by a rim of dirty white light. The light is failing fast.

Once I've installed my last two cameras, I ramble down the stairs. Mary has packed up to go. She nods cordially at me as she picks her handbag off the staircase. 'You'll be fine' she says kindly. 'Now Jane sleeps through here, down the corridor at the back–' she points towards the kitchen '–so if there's anything you need or if anything happens, just give her a shout.' She ties her coat belt tightly around her middle and calls a goodbye behind her. The huge door bangs to, and she is gone.

Skye is upstairs in the library in front of the fire. She is cross-legged, her eyes closed. Mark sees me looking at her. 'Getting in the mood,' he says with a faint smile, adjusting his film camera. 'Attuning to the building.' In the background, a slight, elderly woman – Jane, I presume – is crouched over the fire, which is crackling furiously and emitting sharp bangs. It may be my imagination, but I think I can feel the heat starting to radiate out and minimise the startling cold. I raise my camera and shoot some photographs of Skye. I focus on her pale, freckled face, her almost translucent skin. Jane wanders by me, nods a hello and moves out of the room just as Bill comes in. 'Well, now, y'all' he smiles 'Here we are. All ready to go.' His grin is broad and friendly.

Skye stretches elaborately. 'Thank Christ this room is heating up a little! What are they thinking of, not to bring in heaters? We could get seriously sick here.'

'Oh now,' protests Mark. 'I think we're made of stronger stuff than that.'

She looks down her long, narrow nose at him. 'Fine for

you,' she says coldly. 'But I have lung issues. I need to ensure that I am always at optimum temperature.'

'Right.' Only a polite Englishman could fit so much disbelief into one small syllable.

She ignores him, instead setting out small cushions in a circle. 'I need you all for this bit,' she calls over her shoulder. I look eloquently at Bill and Mark. Mark is openly smirking. In a weird way, it's almost fun, having someone to gang up on. And Skye is truly awful. She continues to bully us, her strident whine cutting across the cold room. 'Now I want you all to sit down, yes, cross-legged if you can. Then I need you to empty your minds of clutter. I want you to focus on the room itself. On the history of the castle. On the presence of the witch, Bridget Ryan. Or, rather *alleged* witch and probable Gaelic healing woman,' she adds piously. I sit down obediently, trying to recall the briefing notes. According to them, the woman, Bridget Ryan, was stoned to death outside the castle in the early nineteenth century for the crime of setting a curse on the landlord's cattle. I look out the window at the bleak landscape and shudder.

'Eyes closed!' This is directed at me. I hastily shut my eyes and to my surprise find the sensation is relaxing. The silence is almost perfect, the tiny wheeze of our breathing the only audible sound. A thin chill breezes up against my face. The vast room is silent. Then, faintly there is a 'ting' like glass being struck lightly, a pause, a footfall, a pause, a light scurry of steps. Skye's eyes pop open instantly, she grabs my sleeve. 'You heard that?'

'Yes,' says Bill, and then, seeing her fright; 'Hey, don't worry, it'll just be that old lady!'

Skye's pupils are dilated. 'Jane!' she calls suddenly.

'Ah, Skye, don't.' I pat her arm. 'Don't call her up all these stairs again.' Skye doesn't listen. 'Come here!' she calls. She is clearly upset, her cheeks and neck are a mottled purple-red.

There is a silence, and then we hear the slow, creeping footsteps come up the stairs. The door creaks open. Jane looks at us, her face uncertain. 'You called me?'

Mark stands up and apologises, tells her it was a mistake. She nods and disappears again. I check my camera, and decide to walk around by myself for a while. *Group hysteria*, I think knowledgeably. I will be safer on my own.

Much later I wander down to the kitchen. Bill is there, stirring soup on the stove. It smells marvellous. 'Here,' he offers, ladling it into a bowl. 'Campbell's finest, ma'am!' I savour the heavy, delicious scent of tomato. Everything is flavoured with a surreal edge of tiredness that makes the panorama of pots and bowls twist and buckle as I yawn.

'So, how you doin' up there?' Bill pours out his own soup.

'Grand,' I reply, stretching my arms above the armchair in a bliss of warmth. My skin is now heated on one side from the open fire, the other still chill to touch.

'No sign of the witch?' He is smiling, but his voice is grave.

'Nothing yet. Those noises were weird, though, earlier. Did anything odd happen when you were working in Tennessee?'

'You could say that,' he says quietly, then pauses. I nod eagerly, mouth full, to encourage him to keep going. 'Well, we were in Bell Witch Cave in Adams, Tennessee – you've heard the story, about how she haunted a farming family there in the early years of the nineteenth century, and, so folks believe, for a long time before that. In fact they say her legend might derive from the Trail of Tears, the dispossession of the native Americans and how their souls haunted the land claimed by the settlers. I grew up round those parts, and I'd been recording in the cave on and off for years. Let me tell you, I heard some weird sounds in that time. But it wasn't till I met Skye that she persuaded me that there might be a whole, big project in it. So we did the filming there. Some strange stuff, alright. Carol wasn't too happy there.' He is almost speaking to himself.

'Carol, the other photographer? The one who dropped out of this project?' He looks at me, an odd sideways glance.

'Yes.'

'She *really* didn't like it,' chimes in Mark from the doorway. Both Bill and I jump.

'Jesus!' I say good-naturedly. 'Don't creep up on us in a haunted castle!' Mark laughs.

'Poor Carol. She claimed it made her feel sick – the place,

the atmosphere. I think she felt that doing it all again here would be too much for her.'

'So did you see anything there?' I am curious.

'Not really,' says Bill, rinsing the soup saucepan with hot water. 'Some shadows. Some odd noises. We went astray for a bit, got disorientated.' He clears this throat, obviously wanting to change the subject. I imagine being with them in the dark cave and shiver. While Bill and Mark discuss the technical details of the US leg of the project, I feel the welcome warmth begin to thaw out my ears and nose. I trace a finger over the worn floral patterns on the armchair, patches faded on the arms to expose rough stitching below. I finish my soup and sigh. 'Right, so, back up the stairs with me, then.'

I go from room to room, checking all the cameras are still on the timers. It's dark now – *dark as the hobs of hell*, as my mother would say. I feel like a proper paranormal investigator as I flash my torch around. Those shows always look so action-packed on TV, with their edited highlights. No-one tells you about the long waits, the intense boredom, and the biting cold. I have positioned myself on the staircase, with a sleeping bag for warmth. One o'clock. Two o'clock. I traipse down every hour to make myself a cup of tea. Bill has set up his equipment but seems to have abandoned it to have a nap in the warmth of the kitchen. I debate joining him, but then am tempted by the thought of getting some more photos. Three o'clock. I'm just shooting a roll of film to capture my torch's reflections on the wooden stairs when several things happen at once.

There is a shout – *Mark?* I think, confused. 'Something bloody touched me! It did!'

It is Mark. I can hear Skye crying downstairs. I freeze, confused, then I hear it, the sound of slow deliberate steps coming down the staircase towards me. I don't even think, I just scream and run, trip-falling, stumbling, running again till I reach the bottom of the stairs.

'Jane!' Skye is sobbing, loud, harsh sobs, as she throws open the kitchen door. 'Oh Jane!'

Mark is just behind us, breathless. He is shaking,

'What the hell?' Bill sits up straight in his chair, dazed, hair crumpled on one side of his face.

The door at the back of the kitchen opens and a girl appears, blinking, in a t-shirt and shorts.

'What's all the bloody noise?' she says in a strong Australian accent. We look at her, then at each other.

'Where's Jane?' blurts out Skye. The girl knuckles her eyes, and frowns, standing with one bare brown foot on top of the other on the rough stone flags.

'I'm Jane,' she says, bewildered.

'What about the old woman? She was up with us earlier in the library?' says Mark. He is clutching his coat around him convulsively.

'Jeez,' says Jane blankly. 'Sorry mates. No-one like that works here.'

And that's how the night ends.

When Mary comes in the morning, we are all in the kitchen, huddled around the fire. Skye is chalk-pale, freckles standing out like marker dots on her face. Mark looks tired and ill, and even Bill is subdued. All of our equipment was gathered up at first light. Mary unbelts her coat and puts on the kettle. She is clearly curious about our night and even asks us about it directly.

'It was great,' I say, 'but we're on a tighter deadline than we anticipated. No time for tea. Thanks for everything.' She says nothing else, but her shrewd glance follows us as we pack up the car.

That's it, I guess. I don't think the project was ever completed. I shared my images with the others on Dropbox as per the agreement. That was the last I heard of the project. I never heard anything about the promised launch. We never collaborated as artists again.

I heard Carol had her baby. A little girl, perfectly healthy. I bumped into her at an exhibition recently, but she didn't want to talk about the Tennessee shoot, just like Mark told me. In fact, when I brought it up, she looked at me like I'd just vomited on her shoes. Then she walked away.

Mark? I have no idea where Mark is. I think he's still based in London, making fastidious, detailed work. I'd say he probably finished his film of Skye's performance, he was that sort of person.

Skye is dead. I saw her obituary notice in a visual arts newsletter. It seems odd that someone so spiky and *present* should be dead. I feel bad. I never really believed in her proclaimed lung condition.

Bill still writes to me, diffidently and intermittently. He never mentions Knocknamara. His occasional emails are comfortable anecdotes of farms and canyons and the sounds he's captured outdoors.

And me? I'm fine, for the most part. I didn't send them all the photos you know. I kept some back. There are some of us in the kitchen, drinking tea, laughing. I like those.

There's a few I don't like. They're the photographs of Skye I took in the library.

Here, look at this one. It's a good portrait, a close-up. I've captured her haughty, patrician face, the atmosphere of stillness she could evoke. I've also captured something else, something that keeps me awake at night. Behind Skye, there is a shadow. Look closer and you can see – if you squint a little – it looks like a dark shape. Look at the next one. Now you can clearly see what it is – an old woman standing by the fire. And in this one – the last photo in the sequence – you can see her wrinkled face in the firelight. She's looking right at Skye, and her face is twisted in a bitter smile.

I can't bring myself to destroy that photo. Sometimes at night I'll take it out and look at it. Who was she? Why did she come to us?

And, on the darkest of nights, I wonder – *can she find us again?*

PAPERING OVER THE CRACKS

On the third day she finds it on the attic wall. She's in the middle of the slow but satisfying ritual of stripping wallpaper; first soaking, and then unpeeling back the thick flaps of flock wallpaper from the green-painted plaster beneath.

Sponge. Pause. Rip.

Pause.

Sponge. Pause. Rip.

Her body moves to the rhythm of the work; some part of her enjoying the mindlessness of it all, a respite from thinking. She slops water on the filthy paper and waits, and then a minute later, a great strip of sodden, muddy wallpaper peels greasily off the wall. She lifts the sponge to apply more water, thinking *I must change the water before it gets too murky* – and then she sees it. For a few seconds she peers at the wall, unable to see what exactly it is, but as she's doing so she leans too far over and loses her balance, knocking the stool and the bucket resting on it. As she swears and starts to mop the water up using an old jumper, heavy steps blunder up the stairs.

'Donna! What is it? Everything OK?'

She sighs, vaguely ashamed. ''S alright, Mark, I just jumped and knocked it over.'

'Idiot,' he says fondly, then pauses, frowning. 'What's that?'

'What's what?' She mops the floor crossly with quick, angry swipes, wanting him to help her, and refusing to ask.

Mark moves closer to the wall. 'That's so weird. It's a face of some kind. Look, I'll clear it.' He grabs the sponge and rubs it over the wall, then rips the paper off awkwardly, leaving fragments of it behind. 'Now look at it!'

She stands up slowly, wiping her hands on the front of her dirty jeans.

'Wow,' she says eventually. They turn to look at each other.

'Is it just me, or does it look a bit…?' Mark's voice tails off, unwilling to voice his thoughts. She traces the outlines on the stained wall with a careful finger.

'It does,' she says. Her voice is flat. 'It looks exactly like me.' She looks at him mutely, her face blank with astonishment.

It was only a month ago that they got the news. When she opened the letter, she was standing stork-like on the doormat, leg tucked against the other in a yoga stance half-remembered from classes years ago. She read it once. Then again. Then she shrieked like an old kettle.

'Mark! MARK! We got it!'

His boots thump-thumped down the stairs. 'We did?'

'It's ours! The dream house! The Georgian mansion of your fantasies!' They hugged, tight and hard, excited, only half-believing the news.

'Now comes the hard part.' Mark disentangled himself. 'The renovations. I'll take a look at those drawings again. We need to go through them closely, work out a master-plan…' His voice trailed off as he pushed his glasses up from his nose on top of his shaven head, a gesture he always made when deep in thought. She hung on to his neck like a scarf.

'But we're happy? Right? This is the house we've always wanted, a lovely Georgian house, my great-aunt's house. And at a great price! We should celebrate!' She wanted to be comforted, applauded.

'Right,' he said absently, a perfunctory smile flickering on and off abruptly. She unwound her arms and released him, knowing she had already lost him to his study, to his precise one-point perspectives, his inked elevations, his minutely detailed floorplans.

It was the kind of house that took you over. *The size is one thing*, thinks Donna – it's an immense Georgian house with four floors, including a basement and attic – *but it's also got an imposing immensity about it that's daunting*. It's also very cold unless the open fires are lit, but Mark is already making noises about unobtrusive underfloor heating that won't disturb the precious symmetry of the elegant interior. When they move in, the first thing Mark does is start to get rid of superfluous furniture: 'to strip the house back to its bare bones,' as he puts it. Great-Aunt Jane was a hoarder. Donna spends the first few days piling up cheap furniture, hideous vases, tatty old newspapers and entire wardrobes of musty clothes into the skip outside.

The dining room, not used at present, becomes a storage room for the remnants of Great-Aunt Jane's possessions that have passed Mark's strict criteria. Slowly, Donna's stealthy additions to these means that the piles start to coalesce and take shape as collection points of colourful miscellanea. These piles grow steadily, day after day, at the same time as the rest of the house is on a slow, inevitable voyage towards a barer, sparer aesthetic. Under Mark's directions, the workmen arrive and pull out the ratty old kitchen units and install appropriate Belfast sinks and simple, minimal cupboards. Mark supervises them carefully, wincing whenever a hammer taps too hard, or a greasy hand smears a surface. His love of Georgian period architecture is one of the things that first attracted her to him, when she wandered into his Design Week talk, lukewarm plastic glass of white wine in hand; the enthusiasm with which he lovingly described the intense harmony and symbolic orders of the architectural style. In his own practice, he prides himself on his popular marriage of classical detailing with modern minimalism. 'The new classicism' is the phrase he uses with clients to describe his style. Secretly Donna feels it a little... soulless, all stripped floors and walls that offer a symphony of chalky whites and dove greys. Her own tastes run more to the Victorian style, to a more feminine and eclectic mode of design. That's why Mark offers her the attic room (far from his exacting gaze) as a place to decorate, a place for her to spend her sabbatical, writing her book. That's why she's preparing her nest at the top of the house. That's why she is stripping the seventies-style wallpaper. And that's how she finds the drawing.

This drawing on the attic wall stirs something within her, a living, impatient curiosity to find out where it has come from. She starts her investigations in the remaining pile of Great-Aunt Jane's possessions. When Mark arrives home, tired and aggressive, like he usually is after his weekly after-work squash bout, she is absorbed in the pile of photo albums found on one of the dusty bookcases.

'What are you doing there?'

She holds up a fan of old photos of the attic room, all oil paintings and bookcases. 'Looking at photos of the house as it was, back in the day.'

'Back in the day? I don't know why you want all that clutter preserved. Old fake-Victorian tat covering up the elegance of the Georgian detailing.' He pulls his mouth sideways into a grimace.

'I'm not one of your bloody clients. You don't need to talk down to me.'

'I'm not talking down to you.'

She rolls her eyes.

'God, you're such a child,' he says contemptuously and walks out. A minute later she hears the *thud-thud* as he kicks off his trainers, and then the spurt and hiss of the power shower upstairs. She feels a sharp dislike of him prickle under her skin, his stupid thick-framed glasses, his sweaty shaven head.

She stays in the room till nearly two o'clock, sifting, opening, reading. And when she goes to bed, she goes to the uncomfortable one in the spare room.

That night she dreams of the drawing, the blank, terrified eyes, the gaping mouth, and wakes up with a heaving start, sitting up straight, wild-eyed and panting.

The next morning she returns to look at the drawing in the attic, again and again, as if to reassure herself of its physical reality. But there it always is, always exactly the same, a full-length drawing of a woman sketched with bursts of brutal energy, deep scores of lead pencil pressed down on the discoloured plaster. It is drawn cleverly to mimic the figure of a woman pressed against a window-pane or some other invisible obstacle, her body flattened, her hands splayed in front of her.

But that isn't the disturbing part. That's the face. Line for line, shadow for shadow, the drawing mimics the curves and hollows of her own face. She sits down at the old writing desk and tries to focus on her manuscript. With the laptop open, she starts a new file and taps out 'Chapter One' in bold type, then stops. Is it her imagination or does the drawing look darker than she remembers? By the time she's finishing a careful examination of the cross-hatched shading, it's time for lunch. She eats a large sandwich downstairs, standing over the sink, reluctant to use a plate that will then have to be stacked (according to Mark) immediately in the dishwasher. It's time now, time to either start writing or start sorting out the oddments and books and possessions in the dining room. That's one of her main jobs, after all. Mark's jobs are more about sitting in his study with the house plans overlaid by his delicate drawings on transparent paper as he reflects on the renovations to come. Writing or sorting? She shrugs and does neither, instead returning to the attic, spending an indolent afternoon watching the shadows crawl and lengthen across the floor. Finally, faintly, in the distance, she hears the front door creak open, and Mark call her name.

Mark is annoyed with her. She can tell it by his carefully-neutral expression as he sits at the kitchen table; she knows it by the set of his shoulders (hunched, tense) and the precise, irritable way he lays down his knife and fork beside his plate. He has grazed his hand while moving in some boxes to the hall, and has wrapped it up, ostentatiously, like a visible symbol of reproach. She isn't in the mood to fight; instead she moves around the kitchen, restoring order, completing their ancient, placatory rituals, pouring him a glass of white wine, straightening the place settings. Now she's at the old Aga, quietly stirring the pot of green curry, unwilling to provoke him into the tirade she feels brewing, ominous and inevitable as a rising wave. When they start eating, she silently counts the seconds in her head until he starts to speak. At fifty-six seconds he breaks the silence.

'It's not that I'm complaining,' he begins (although, patently, he is). She stays quiet and keeps forking up the curry. 'It's just that we're meant to be a team here, working together to get this renovation done.' He glares at her through his black-rimmed glasses, which she is perversely glad to see, are steaming up with the vapour of the food on his plate.

'Okay,' she says quietly.

'I mean, it's not every day you find something weird like

that drawing in the attic, but for God's sake, get over it and help me out a bit. We've got the whole huge house to work on.' He drinks his wine noisily.

'Okay.' She rams a large forkful of curry in her mouth to choke down her agreement and prevent any further discussion.

'Good.' He lays a hand on hers, in a gesture meant to be reassuring. Her skin itches in annoyance.

The next day she even takes a mirror up with her so she can compare them both; herself and the drawing. What was incomparable though is the expression on the two faces. While her real-life reflection stares back in pallid surprise, her blanched face looking pale and unwieldy, the face of her drawn doppelganger is urgent, startling, the eyes mute with misery. The mouth is a big O of gaping horror, the dark expanse within it cross-hatched with savage black lines. In between these bouts of contemplation, over the next few days she continues to slowly strip the wallpaper in the room, careful as a mortician, but underneath reveals nothing more than dirt, ancient insect mummies and damp marks.

The drawing has become all-important. Its physical presence in the house acts like a magnetic current for her thoughts, drawing them endlessly back to the attic room. Every day, without fail, as soon as Mark leaves for work, she spends the day in the attic. Every day she goes back to the dining room, and, using the old photographs as a guideline, she selects objects from the pile and brings them upstairs. Slowly, stealthily, she starts to restore the attic to its former glory.

It becomes a challenge, an obsession. From the letters and photographs, she builds an idea of how the attic had been constructed during her great-aunt's tenure. She moves the bookcases up during the daytime, and puts her own books on the shelves, taking time to place them neatly together, organised by colour. And so she passes the afternoons up there, sitting, reading and just looking at the drawing on the wall.

#

At this stage she hasn't even bothered to pretend to help with any of the work around the house, pleading the need to work on her book. Today Mark has gone to IKEA to get some essentials. He had asked her repeatedly to come, but she refused: 'Too much paperwork to sort out,' she lied. He grabbed his keys, scraping them angrily against the countertop. Minutes later she heard the car engine blast on, a thin squealing distress call of rubber, and the sound of his car driving fast and hard down the road. She sits quietly till the sound of the car faded away, then goes upstairs, her socked feet treading lightly on the wooden stairs, as if Mark can somehow hear her betrayal. Then she's back in her refuge. Thanks to her hard work, the attic room is now reconstructed to her satisfaction. The bookshelves are complemented by an elderly chaise longue heaped with floral cushions, a thin old Persian carpet, worn but colourful, and a writing desk with mismatched wooden chair.

She stands in front of the drawing again. Is it her imagination or does it look a little different today? The eyes seem more anguished than ever. She touches it again, lightly, and wishes she had someone to ask to come over and look at it. But she doesn't; the downsides of moving to a new neighbourhood. She runs a delicate finger over the whorls and curlicues of the lead pencil and wonders again – *who is she?*

That night she calls her mother. It doesn't happen often, her mother doesn't like Mark, and the feeling is mutual. But he's working late, so he's not there to witness her traitorous act. Her mother sounds mildly surprised to hear from her. She brushes past the usual questions and gets straight to the point.

'What do you know about Great-Aunt Jane? I mean, I never met her as a child.'

'No. No, you wouldn't have.'

'Was she…' I cast about for a handy euphemism. 'A bit odd?'

Her mother laughs, a short, unexpected laugh. 'She was that alright. Never really saw anyone or appeared at any family events. Loved her home, no children, never even married. Never really left the house until the end. That's all I know really.'

#

It's nearly September, she thinks. *Normally I should be getting ready for work.* She's overcome with an intense, almost indulgent sense of lassitude, the luxury of an earned sabbatical. She remembers, as if it were another lifetime, her usual sequence of meetings that normally mark the end of the summer, the preparation of lecture notes and the panic shopping for work clothes. She thinks again about her book, those unopened folders on her attic desk. Idly, she thinks about her book proposal, her grandiose plans, that now all seem faintly absurd, irrelevant, unimportant. Instead she lies on the chaise longue and drinks tea, and just watches the drawing, watches the sun pattern the walls until the shadows fall, until the car-lights turn into the driveway, and it's time to return reluctantly downstairs.

One day her mother rings. At first she doesn't answer (the phone, after all, is down two flights of stairs). But the shrilling tone continues until she can't ignore it anymore. Eventually she picks up. Her mother seems distracted.

'I was thinking about our last chat,' she says, without preamble. 'Can we meet for coffee? This morning? If you're not too busy with your book,' she adds humbly. The fact her daughter writes books is a never-ending source of amazement for her. Donna thinks about her blank notebooks and silent laptop upstairs, and feels the beginnings of an ancient guilt stirring.

'Sure thing,' she says, and then looks down at her pyjama legs. 'Just give me half an hour to get ready. Usual place?'

It feels... strange... to be outside, out in the world. *So noisy,* she thinks, *so many fast-moving people and cars*. She feels herself shrink back against the chair in the coffee-shop. Her mother notices, and puckers her lips with a worried twist of her mouth.

'How are you doing, Donna dear?'

'Fine.' She fiddles with her spoon.

Her mother perseveres. 'I hope that big house isn't too much for you. It's an awful lot to take on.' The concerned tone of her voice soothes Donna like a sweet balm. She decides to tell her.

'I found something in the attic.' She flicks through the photos on her phone until she finds one of the images she took of the drawing. 'Here, what do you think of that?'

Her mother stares at it, then at Donna, then back at the screen again.

'Oh,' she says faintly. She covers her mouth in an oddly old-fashioned gesture. Donna almost feels an urge to laugh, but her mother's expression stops the desire in its tracks. Her mother's face is almost grey, her lips bloodless. Quickly, she pours her more tea, adds sugar and offers her the cup. Her mother takes it, sips, then puts it down.

'I'm sorry,' she says faintly. 'It's quite a shock. Is that something Mark drew? Of you? And why?'

'It's *not* a drawing of me. That's the weird thing. I found it under the wallpaper in Great-Aunt Jane's attic.'

'In the attic?' Donna nods.

'That's where she was, all the time...' her mother's voice drifts off, and then resumes, a little louder and stronger. 'Aunt Jane. We would be taken to visit her as children. She was old then, and wasn't well, and we had to go up all those flights of stairs to the attic bedroom. She'd be in bed, with all her things around her, vases and cushions and chairs and paintings.' She peers closer. 'But I don't remember that.' She pats her daughter's hand and then passes back the phone, photograph still on the screen. 'A coincidence of course, but a nasty shock, all the same to find that. I hope you and Mark weren't too upset by it.'

'I was shocked, but now I'm more curious. Mark thinks I should forget about it. You know Mark.' Donna smiles, a quick, twisted smile, tight at the edges. Her mother looks at her with compassion.

'He's a bully,' she says quietly. 'Your father was the same.' Her eyes are brown and sorrowful as an old dog.

When she goes home, she rehearses her conversation again. She drifts into the dining room and its landscape of odd-ments. Today she's going through old correspondence. Most of it turns out to be bills and formally written cards, but there's an interesting letter tucked under a pile of yellowing lace doilies. The first page is missing but the rest is intriguing. It makes frequent reference to illness and talks lovingly about the attic room as a 'retreat'. The signature is a flowing copperplate 'Jane'. Her great-aunt. Donna sits back on her heels and frowns. Now she knows what rang strange earlier in her mother's description of being in the house. *Surely if she were an invalid,* she thinks, *wouldn't she have been on the ground floor?* She puts the letter back carefully and goes back to the attic. There's no point in doing anything else, it's now late afternoon and Mark will be back soon. They've pretty much given up all pretence that she is helping with the house, but she needs at least to have an open notebook on her desk to fool both of them that she is making progress on her book. And all goes well until he comes home.

'Jesus Christ!' Mark stands in the attic doorway. His face crinkles in disgust. 'This is where all the tat has migrated to!' She sits up in her chair and looks defensively around her room, her precious cosy retreat, with its dark green walls, its old-fashioned portraits, its layered surfaces and contrasting furniture.

'I like it like this.'

'But *Architectural Digest* are coming to photograph the house!' His voice is almost a wail. At the back of her mind she knows this is a huge thing for Mark, an announcement he's practiced making to her, but her resentment flows dark and fast.

'They don't need to come up here,' she says shortly. 'You said I could have this room. Well, this is the way I like it!'

His mouth closes in an ugly line. He looks around, and then points at her laptop.

'What's that?' It's her open laptop screen, the words 'Chapter One' standing black and stark on an empty white page. His face is a study of disbelief.

'All this time I've been working, and you've...' He catches his breath, too angry to continue. He puts his hands to his head and closes his eyes. When he speaks again, it is in a carefully controlled way.

'Have you written anything yet?'

'My sabbatical is for the whole term.' She can't even remember the last time she even thought about the book.

He looks around the room again. 'All this time...'

Suddenly she can't bear that supercilious look on his face, his ineffable rightness. She gets up.

'And where are you going?'

'To my mother's.' She faces him, defiant. '*She* likes to spend time with me.'

'I'm glad you came over.'

Donna hasn't really said anything about the fight, that silly fight, but her restful mother knows, just knows without demanding details. Instead they spend the evening sharing the Chinese takeaway Donna brought over. 'Far too much for me, and the *expense*! You must bring back the leftovers.' They sit down together with a pot of tea to watch an old episode of *Morse*. Donna breathes in with an audible sigh. The air is heavy with a kind of somnolent contentment that she rarely finds in her own home, except for in her attic room. She thinks of it now, her room with Mark standing in it, his face of disgust, and shakes her head hard to rid herself of the vision.

'Anything the matter?' Her mother has paused *Morse*, a significant act. She cocks her head at Donna, a mute invitation to confide.

'Actually, there's something I want to ask you.' Donna hears herself say. 'Do you have any photos of Great-Aunt Jane?' Her mother nods.

It takes a while, a rummage through the photo albums and a trawl through the boxes in the spare room, but her mother finally finds them.

'Here.' She spreads out some old black and white photos, their edges curled and tobacco-coloured.

Donna has the queerest feeling, a lightness and a heaviness all at once, as if her stomach has flipped over inside her. She points. 'That's her.'

Her mother peers closer. 'Yes, that's right.' She squints at it again. 'And you can see the family resemblance.' It's more than a resemblance. Cold sweat prickles on Donna's back. Great-Aunt Jane is an older version of herself. An older version of the drawing behind the wallpaper. Same eyes, same hairline, same nose. Different smile… but who can see a smile when the face is distorted in a scream?

She clears her throat, not trusting herself to speak. When she does, she asks, as neutrally as possible, 'What happened to her that she ended up living up in that attic room?'

The evening darkens outside the window as her mother tells her what she remembers of the story.

'We were always told she was sick. Really sick. I told you, I remember being brought up to see her, when she was in bed upstairs. She used to read a lot, and draw, but she didn't speak a lot.'

'What was she sick with?'

'I've no idea. Families didn't really discuss things like that back then. If people had a certain type of sickness, it was rude to discuss it. Unless they died. But poor old Jane just lingered on.' Her face is soft with memories.

'A certain kind of sickness?'

Her mother makes a flapping motion with one hand. 'You know.' Despite the fact that only the two of them are there, she mouths the next two words silently. '*Mental illness*. She wasn't well in the head. Something happened when she was younger, I think. Anyhow, she stayed upstairs, and only the family ever visited her. That's why no-one could believe it when she finally left. No, I'm not sure where she went to,' she adds in response to Donna's unspoken question. 'Maybe it was a nursing home. Maybe it was to a friend's house. Or a relative's?' She frowns, unable to remember which.

And that is all that she can remember. Donna spends a wakeful night in her mother's cluttered spare room, thinking of her great-aunt's lonely, confined life. She is miserably conscious of the comparative richness of her own – her job, her book, her freedom, even Mark.

In the morning she rings him. 'I'm sorry,' he says instantly when he picks up the phone, and she feels a kind of happiness bloom inside her at the rapidity of his response. He is busy finishing a job, he says, and then he'll cook a late afternoon brunch for both of them.

'Truce?'

Mark is holding up a steaming coffee-pot when she opens the kitchen door. It smells delicious, earthy and chocolatey. Her stomach rumbles. And scrambled eggs! Her favourite, the buttery, runny kind.

'Truce,' she agrees happily.

He pulls up a chair for her, and the tiny gesture thrills her with its unspoken consideration. 'I know this move has been difficult for you. I know it's not easy to write when there's builders coming and going. I know that this house has been shaped by the way I want it to be.' She nods, mouth full of hot scrambled egg. 'But I want you to know that it's important for me that we both enjoy the house.'

'Thanks Mark.' She is oddly pleased to be acknowledged, to have him look her in the eye and confirm that her tastes are different to his. He is smiling at her now, almost tenderly, as he watches her eat.

'Aren't you having any?'

'I'll eat later. Afterwards.'

'After what?'

He grins. 'There's a surprise after this!'

She swallows a forkful of creamy egg, and then puts her fork down. 'I can eat later too. What's this surprise?'

'You need to follow me for that.' And she does, out of the kitchen, up the first flight of stairs, the second. On the landing he pauses, then mounts the next flight. He climbs up that one and the next too. Then he puts his foot on the stairs to the attic, and smiles at her. She smiles back uncertainly, but her stomach pitches with a low foreboding at its pit, a feeling that only increases as he strides in front of her with his heavy steps, *thud, thud, thud,* all the way up the stairs, all the way to her attic door.

'I did this yesterday evening. And this morning. Look!' He throws the door open and she sees, to her disbelief, that he has completely made over her room in tasteful Victoriana, in shades of dove and burgundy, with gold accents. The shabby old furniture has been replaced by glossy antiques. The old rug is gone, in its place is a thick, lush Morris print, a lily one that contrasts tastefully with the intertwined bird patterns on the new curtains. Even the walls – she presses her fingers to her mouth – even the walls have been changed. They've been wallpapered with a careful, tasteful brownish-grey paper decorated with an elegant golden lily motif that sparkles at the top of the walls. She moves her hand away from her mouth to the wall, to the place where the drawing was; the gesture is oddly like a kiss of farewell.

It is too much. She's can't speak.

'Well?' Mark is watching her, impatient for reaction. 'I took on board what you wanted. Everything here is properly authentic, to recreate that Victorian look you like so much.' He looks around critically. 'And it's no harm to have an oddity when *Architectural Digest* come to photograph the house – it's something that recognises the different time periods that have played out here.'

It's that last sentence that enrages her, that reference to the *real* inspiration behind the renovation, that forces the bitter words out of her mouth.

'I don't believe you! I liked it just the way it was! With Great-Aunt Jane's pieces here!'

He is shocked. 'But this is much better. It's properly Victorian.'

'Oh my GOD! Only better by YOUR standards!' Now she is crying, openly. 'I loved this little room. It was a proper link to her, to my family. Now it's all gone, probably in a skip somewhere.' His suddenly guilty face tells her this is true. 'You covered up her drawing! You got rid of her things! And replaced it all with this soulless stuff.' She grabs at a minute pucker in the wallpaper and pulls it wildly. It rips in her hand, exposing some of the scrawled lines of the drawing beneath. Donna heaves in a breath and drops her voice in a mean, angry tone. 'You're meant to be an architect, to have a feel for houses. Well this is like some kind of insipid doll house reproduction. You got rid of everything authentic.' She starts crying again, big, ungainly, childlike sobs.

On the periphery of her vision, she sees Mark, too angry to reply, raise his hand and clench it – for a second she starts – then he smashes his fist into the wooden doorframe. He sucks at his sore fist, pauses, opens his mouth, and then closes it again. There's no need to speak. His look of blank, black hate says it all.

She meets his gaze squarely. 'I'm leaving,' she says quietly.

He doesn't reply. His angry steps crash down, down, down, all the way down to the kitchen, where, in the sudden silence of the house she hears the distant 'ping' of the microwave as he heats up the leftover eggs. She hates him then, really hates him for his endless pragmatism, his stubborn, cold practicality. She climbs into the chilly, slippery embrace of one of the new armchairs and sobs herself quiet.

Donna stays in that room, eyes sore from crying, until the shadows streak over the floor. It gets colder and darker, until her bare T-shirted arms are stiff with goose-pimples, ridges of them. She rubs her arms and stands up, chilled and aching, her hip popping slightly as she does so.

'If only I could go back,' she says wistfully, thinking of the room as it was, with all its familiar signposts, the drawing on the wall and the comfortable, shabby furnishing. Gripped by a superstitious moment, she even closes her eyes as she says it. When she opens them, of course, all is as it was, a pristine, beautiful, lifeless evocation of a Victorian room.

She barely remembers going downstairs, just the sensation of weight and comfort as she slides, fully-dressed, between the heavy duvet in the spare room. Her hot eyes flicker closed, soothed by the cool cotton surface of the pillow.

It is a strange night, full of half-sleeps and part-dreams, a bustling, disturbed kind of night full of sounds and movement, through which she moves, half-waking, never fully sleeping.

It's morning now. But it's dark. I can't see anything. The duvet must have wrapped itself round me, it's tight, so tight that I can't move. I try to move, but I can't, I'm so securely pinned down. Even my head is constricted; I feel my mouth opening, trying to pull in a breath in this airless darkness. My hands push against the duvet, but it's not yielding. Dimly, at the corner of my eye, I can see a glow, a crack of light, and beyond it...

This makes no sense! I can see a tiny sliver beyond it, but it's nothing from the familiar landscape of the spare room. This is something different, a minute fragment of brownish-grey, flecked with gold.

And then I understand it all. I can't scream, though my mouth is open. I'm trapped here, no matter how much I try to call for help, no matter how hard I press my hands against the band that constricts me. I am flat and silenced and invisible.

There's no help on the way. Mark will just think I've left. He won't think to look for me.

He won't think to look for me here.

Behind the wallpaper.

TWO FACED

She stood in the crisp sunlight, feeling the wind tug at her hair. Everywhere she turned, there was Vienna, ostentatious and perfect as a wedding cake. The Hofburg Palace lay before them, sparkling white in the cold air, gigantic curving walls opened in an embrace.

'Wow,' she breathed, hand going automatically for her camera.

Alex made an irritated noise. 'Jesus, its freezing!'

'Yes, but look at it, it's fantastic.'

Another sigh. 'Can we at *least* get in out of the cold?' He marched on ahead, pulling his jacket around his ribs ostentatiously. Kate followed slowly, pausing to photograph an enormous marble sculpture of a heroic nude restraining a rearing horse, the pull of muscle and sinew perfectly tense and frozen. She trotted after him, wishing, as always, that he didn't walk so quickly.

'Aren't the streets amazing?' she asked, breathing heavily. 'I mean, no matter which direction you look, you see some fantastic building in the distance. Great architecture.'

'I suppose,' said Alex, pausing to consider. 'Though it's very same-y, endless classical rip-offs, kind of boring, much like I imagine St. Petersburg to be.' Kate subsided, some of her enthusiasm leaking away. *But it's beautiful,* she thought rebelliously. *And I'm not going to let you spoil it for me.* She gazed up at a stone Adonis hoisting up a doorway on one elegant shoulder. His blank eyes were almond-shaped, his petal-shaped lips drooping, his expression melancholy. *It's not just classical, it's so romantic. Not that you'd understand that concept.*

They faced each other over the café table in the Kunsthistoriches Museum. She smiled in quick delight at the old-fashioned tables, and the jewelled mosaics overhead. The dessert trolley passed by, festooned with elaborate cakes and their nut-sculptured toppings. Alex hunched over the menu.

'There is *nothing* here,' he said flatly. 'Nothing I'd want to eat.' Kate felt suddenly on edge. Did this mean they had to continue walking round Vienna hopelessly, trying to find somewhere that was non-smoking, served bland, meat-and-carbohydrate meals and met with Alex's restaurant-review standards of cleanliness? She picked up her menu and started to hunt in panic for something, anything that he might eat.

'There's spaghetti Bolognese?' she offered with a tight smile. 'You like that.' Her tone was artificially bright, as if talking to a small child. He sighed.

'I suppose so. It'll have to do.' She felt herself curl up inside, withered by his sullen face.

Unbidden, her comfort-image came to mind, a cosy sitting room with her prints on the wall, her books on the bookcase. She was snuggled into the depths of a big leather armchair, with no-one to worry about, eating a plate of the macaroni cheese that Alex hated, watching the soaps that he despised. This was her recurring fantasy, one she had dreamed over, adding layer after layer, like a computer-game designer, making textures more touchable, sensations more vivid. In her head she could smell the sweet, smoky scent of turf briquettes burning and see the brown glazed teapot with the cracked lid, warming by the fireplace. She imagined the lamplight spilling over the floor, gilding the wood.

They were in the Heiligenkreuz monastery, a bus trip, a last attempt to do something interesting. The trip there had been OK; they'd even sniggered slightly over the drawn-out punctuation of the tour guide who seemed to have a crush on 'Crown Prince Rud-olf', obsessing over his 'su-i-cide' in 'Mey-er-ling.' And the road through the Vienna Woods had been charming. She'd tried over and over again to try and capture the scene from the bus, the still darkness of the coniferous trees, before finally giving up. The monastery itself was enchanting. The corridors led to strange, unexpected sights, an elaborate stained-glass window in one niche and an enormous, green-encrusted baptismal font in another. She wandered down the darker recesses of the passageway, peering into a darkened room with a velvet rope hung over the doorway, and jerked back in surprise. It was a tiny chapel, with a table in the centre, surrounded by the bizarre sight of four life-sized skeletons in monks' robes holding candlesticks aloft over their bony heads.

'Ah, this is the mort-u-ary chapel.' It was the unmistakable pronunciation of the tour guide behind her. 'Where the dead monks are laid out. The candlesticks remind us of this.' Kate smiled widely in sheer pleasure at the strangeness of the sight. *How weirdly beautiful,* she thought dreamily. *And how typical of Vienna and its cult of death.* She felt someone brush by her back as she tried to take a photo of the chapel. Too dark. Already she was wondering if she could get a postcard of the candlesticks.

She got back on the bus, feeling her face relax into a smile. It had been a good day, no rows. Alex had even seemed to look interested during the trip. She sat down, feeling a weight slide off her chest, flicking through her postcards.

'Well, I loved that.' A feeling of optimism made her confident enough to add, 'Did you enjoy it?'

Alex raised his eyebrows. 'Well, to be honest, it was a bit boring. A long bus ride for very little.' She felt a wave of despair. 'Although that chapel was cool.'

Kate barely heard him. Her shoulders slumped. A queer, weak feeling swam over her. 'Oh *God!*' The cry came out of her, from the pit of her stomach. 'Nothing I ever do is right. I just wanted you to have a good time. All I *ever* bloody want is for you to have a good time.' Covering her face with her hands she stopped fighting. In the darkness of her hands, she thought *I will never forget how you made me feel right now; how hopeless, how sad.* Dimly she sensed an arm over her shoulders. Her body, stiffened, rejecting it.

She felt the weight of the last endless months of nervous, placatory attempts to dispel his gloom. It was that dull, leaden gloom that drained her joy, and which darkened everything around it. Behind her hands, the yellow light of her imaginary cottage shone like a beacon. Suddenly, desperately, she wanted to be there. Like a leg breaking, like a door slamming, she felt it. It was over. *My ex-husband.* She tried out the phrase in her head. It was terrifying, but plausible.

#

Lauren. *Lauren*. He said her name silently, secretly, like a good-luck charm. He pictured her brown skin, her dark, laughing eyes, the graceful way she crossed her legs, elegant in their pin-sharp heels. Her husky, French-tinted accent played in his head, on a loop. *Oh Alexander, how funny you are!*

God, it was cold. Those empty wide streets and squares acted as wind tunnels, blowing cold air in the faces of the pedestrians. His eyes watered, and he had a sudden, vivid vision of his outer dermis flaying off in the ice-wind, like a nineteenth century medical illustration. The sight of Kate cut through his thoughts. Her dark hair was whipped into wild curls by the wind, her cheeks pink and eyes starry as she gazed around the cold square. With a lurch of irritation he noticed she was wearing the old navy raincoat he hated, the one that swallowed her shape, turning her into a shiny plastic bundle. Frowning, he saw her reach for her camera. If he'd known then how much her perpetual photographing of architectural details would annoy him, he would never have bought her the goddamned thing. It made her look like such a nerdy tourist. His conscience jolted him. It wasn't Kate's fault that she was so... ordinary compared to Lauren. He hunched his shoulders and slowed down to let her catch up with him.

Why did the Viennese have to smoke everywhere? They'd been walking round the city looking for a non-smoking restaurant for so long; he was almost past the stage of being hungry. Lauren had once told him about a weekend she had spent in Budapest with her ex-boyfriend. 'It was thrill-eng,' she had said, smiling slyly. 'For the whole time we nevair left the hotel room, except to buy wine and fresh bread and fruit for the picnics in our room. You should try it.' Alex had laughed and nodded, mind filling with images of Lauren, immaculate bob disordered, wrapped in a white bed-sheet and lobbing grapes at an Action-Man-perfect lover. And then, inevitably, with images of himself replacing the anonymous man, leaning over, filling their glasses with champagne.

But instead of that romantic vision, here he was walking round endless white-pillared streets that acted as wind tunnels, peering into unappetizing café after unappetizing café.

'I'm sorry,' said Kate nervously. 'Perhaps we should go back to the Hofburg, there's a museum café, would that be OK?' His skin prickled with irritation. He nodded curtly, striding past her.

They faced each other over the café table in the Kunsthistoriches Museum. As he had expected, a truly unappealing assortment of food – revolting -sounding Viennese 'specialties' and everything else tarted up with 'leaves' and 'jus'. He sighed. She looked at him nervously. When had Kate stopped being fun? Why did she look so harassed, so pained all the time? She drained the fun out of everything with her endless questions – Are you OK? Is this restaurant alright for you? What do you want to do now? *What if Lauren was here?* he thought suddenly, disloyally. He pictured them holding hands, kissing, laughing over the terrible menu options.

'There's spaghetti Bolognese? You like that, don't you?' Her uncertain tone made him grit his teeth.

'I suppose so,' he said, unable to keep the sulky tone out of his voice. 'It'll have to do.'

They were in the Heiligenkreuz monastery, a bus trip, a last attempt to do something interesting. With the exception of a truly saccharine cassette of Strauss party-piece waltzes, the trip had been fairly enjoyable. Kate and he had even talked, him determinedly pushing thoughts of Lauren to the back of his mind, to try and be fair. It was only when she started taking multiple photos (of *trees*, for Christ's sake) that he felt his patience slip slightly.

The monastery was interesting, dark chapels, old stone carvings. He wandered about, half-listening to the guide. Kate was wandering down the arcaded passage, looking in the apertures and doorways, one hopeful hand on her camera. He examined a large crucifix, with its sorrowful blood-spattered Jesus, when he heard her gasp. Mildly intrigued, he turned around. She was staring in delight at four huge candlesticks, each in the form of a skeletal monk.

'Ah,' said the tour guide, pleased at her reaction. 'This is the mort-u-ary chapel, where the dead monks are laid out. The candlesticks remind us of this.' Alex looked over at Kate. She was smiling that radiant, warm Kate-smile that had first made him love her, the one that filled her whole face, made her eyes crinkle up. Alex felt his heart turn over slightly. Slowly he reached out and touched the back of her raincoat, feeling a sudden, indulgent fondness for its shabby practicality.

'Do you want to go the gift shop before we get on the coach?' he asked. He knew she had an inordinate fondness for those tacky shops and was probably already secretly itching to buy a monk-skeleton keyring.

'Sure, yes, but you don't have to. See you on the coach?' He watched her scuttle off, mind already straying back to what Lauren had said before he left for Vienna.

'Hmm, what kind of men do I like?' She pretended to ponder the answer, in response to his oh-so-casual question. 'Well, Alexander, usually men who are tall and dark, like you. Maybe I should ask Kate if I can borrow you?' Her eyes were wicked. She laughed, but the invitation in her smile was unmistakable. He felt the breath catch, sharply, in his chest. A queer giddiness filled him, like helium. Retreating back to the safety of his office, he couldn't resist an exultant, whispered 'Yessssss!' And he'd thought then – *When I get back from holiday, you can borrow me alright!* Mind filling pleasurably with this image, he looked up from his seat on the bus. Kate was making her way down the aisle, grinning and waving postcards at him. She sat down beside him.

'Look, I got one of the candlesticks. They were divine! I want one so much…' Her voice trailed off happily as she shuffled the images like a deck of cards.

Turning she said, 'Well, I loved that. Did you enjoy it?' It was the slightly worried way she added the last sentence that grated.

'Well, to be honest, it was a bit boring. A long bus ride for very little.' He saw her face falling and tried to make amends. 'Although that chapel was cool.'

'Oh *God!*' Her voice was raised. He felt the shock show on his face. 'Nothing I *ever* do is right. I just wanted you to have a good time. All I ever bloody want is for you to have a good time.' She wept, silently. Looking at Kate sitting beside him, her hands at her eyes, her dark hair falling over her face like a curtain to hide her tears, suddenly Alex felt unutterably moved. A wave of affection rose in him for her, for her endless desire to please him, her patient love. He put an awkward arm around her. His irritating, well-meaning wife.

It would be all right. Everything would be all right.

89

PERFECT PITCH

Thank you so much for coming here today. We know you will be as excited about this possibility as we are. I run the beginning of the pitch over and over in my head as I lie on the miniscule bed in room 206. I am glad to shut the door between myself and London, with all its noise and largeness and rush. 'Thank you so much for coming here today,' I mouth to myself. Should I add, *'We really appreciate that you've travelled this distance?'* Or will that make him aggrieved? Remind him that we've made him travel? I've looked it up. According to the internet it is almost eleven hours, non-stop. That's OK, I think. I wouldn't mind it. Eleven hours in business class would be no problem.

I look around the room. It is tiny. It is more than tiny. It is, I suspect, a converted cupboard. I am lying on the smallest single bed in London. Bolted to the wall at the bottom of my bed is a tiny TV. Underneath is a hook. My suit hangs neatly on it. When I half-close my eyes, it looks like someone is standing at the foot of my bed. There is a minute nightstand with a phone and a bathroom cubicle that barely fits a toilet and a shower. But it's cheap, it's central, and I'm only here for two nights. Le Grand is due to step off his aircraft at around two o'clock. Then he'll come here, I'll make my pitch, we'll chat and I'll take him out for dinner. I have planned the restaurant. A Lebanese restaurant, just two streets away. I've researched the meze options so I can talk him through them, from hummus and halloumi to the more obscure dishes like *sojok* (spicy sausages) and *samboussik lahme* (a pastry with lamb and pine nuts). I feel confident to advise him. I don't expect him to be a vegetarian, but if he is, there is an extensive range of meat-free dishes. Everything is in order. One of the helpful Asian men from the reception area has helped me set up the small conference room with the projector and the seating. I've already run through my PowerPoint presentation a few times; now the words and images from the slides are ticking through my brain. I look at my watch. Nine pm. I've caught the early flight, and feel the ache of tiredness in my back

and legs. I'm tempted to sink further into the uncomfortable bed and drift into a half-sleep, but I resist. I need to ring
Debs anyway.

Debs. Deborah. I think of her as I pass through the reception, by the vending machine, the front desk – 'Hello!'
'Hello!'– and down the flight of steps to the road. The hotel
is painted in the same cream colour as all the other buildings
on the road – a neat Victorian terrace of small townhouses,
with only a discreet sign proclaiming it as 'The Court
Hotel' differentiating it from its fellows. Once outside the
air is cool and inviting as I walk down to the main street.
Deborah, I think. I check my watch again. Not too late to
call. My phone is a work phone and obstinately refuses to
function when outside Ireland. Something to do with data
roaming charges and my lack of seniority. It's quite discon-
certing not to have it with me. I feel like I have lost a watch,
a computer, the internet and a camera all in one. I need to
queue at reception for the one 'business customer' computer
in order to check my email. *Like a time-traveller back to the
1990's*, I think and smile. But I need to ring her. I have no
idea where I'll find a phone box, but instinct tells me to
check the main street.

I frown as I walk. Last night was distinctly odd. I was
mulling over my presentation, flicking through slides on
my laptop at the kitchen table. I knew Debs was in a bad
mood. I could hear her crashing the dishes into the dishwasher. Normally she is deft and noiseless. I felt I should ask
her what was wrong, but I was pretty sure that she was just
annoyed that I was 'swanning off' (as she'd termed it earlier)
to London without her. When I went up to bed she was
already there, her back an immobile lump in the darkness.
She didn't respond to my whisper, or my arm across her hip,
so I withdrew it and lay on my back, looking at the ceiling
and willing myself to sleep before the alarm went off.

I stand outside a branch of Pret-A-Manger and study the
terrain. The streets are busy as always, even on this summer's
night. I marvel at the diversity of the hurrying throng, West
African women in traditional robes, a Sikh man with a long
white beard and majestic turban, a gaggle of Japanese girls
armed with cameras and Hello Kitty merchandise. There is a
phone box there – outside the Tube entrance, by the frozen

yoghurt shop. But when I draw closer I smile at my mistake. It is a replica of the old Tardis-style police boxes, its dusty exterior full of finger-drawn Doctor Who graffiti. I try the handle, just in case, but the box is firmly locked. I give up, and buy a frozen yoghurt instead from an Australian man who directs me helpfully to the nearest phone booth. It is, confusingly, right back down the street I have just walked down.

'Hello?'

'Debs? It's me.'

'Oh.' *That is an unfriendly 'Oh',* I think but I persevere anyway. 'So I'm all set up here, waiting for the meeting tomorrow. The hotel is OK, but the room is tiny. There's a single bed that I swear is smaller than a child's cot.' I elaborate on this so she realises the impossibility of her being invited on this trip.

'Right. That's good you're there anyway.' She is not even listening to me. 'I got you some perfume at the duty free,' I add hopefully. (I didn't, of course. This is a lie. But I can pick some up on the way home). Standing in this dirty phone box, covered in the old-fashioned cards advertising, I am suddenly, weirdly homesick, homesick for her, no matter how spiky she is being, for the feel of the old leather sofa under me at the end of the day, for the Game of Thrones theme tune that signals a truce and popcorn on Monday nights. 'Great,' she says, voice flat and cold. 'I'll see you the day after tomorrow.' She is gone, without wishing me luck. I still have a handful of change, so I call Michael, my boss. He is surprised to hear from me.

'Is everything OK?' he asks anxiously.

'Yes, yes, yes.' I am full of reassurance. 'Everything's in place. It's all ready.' There is a pause.

'Did you have a reason to call me, other than that?' I am miserably aware that this was an unnecessary phone call.

'Nothing else,' I say cheerily. 'Just to let you know there are no hitches. I'm ready for him tomorrow.'

'Good, thanks. Good work,' he says, and I feel obscurely better.

I am back at the hotel. I try to sleep but the little room is warm and humid. I lie in the darkness and listen to footsteps above me, voices heard dimly through walls, the odd burst of TV noise from a distance. I am finding it hard to keep the pitch out of my head, I have practiced it so many times today. *Click on laptop remote for first slide. 'Thank you so much for coming here today. We know you will be as excited about this possibility as we are.' Click on laptop remote to show the second slide.* I turn in bed, restlessly. Breakfast. Preparation. Arrival. Presentation. Chat. Dinner. A drink? – I have settled on a very traditional Victorian English pub, further down the high street, busy but not too busy, historic but sparklingly clean. I try and stop thinking – have you ever tried it? – impossible. I give in and half-listen to the soundscape of voices and traffic, and before I know it, the blind is bleached with sunshine, and it's time to get ready.

8am. Le Grand is still in the clouds. I dress in yesterday's clothes for breakfast. No point in risking an unfortunate spillage on the suit. Breakfast is in the basement, a set of small tables and chairs crowded into an ill-lit room. I load my plate with croissants, fruit and muffins, suddenly, startlingly hungry. All around me are a group of men, Irish men, by their accents. They're about my age, but weather-beaten, with red faces and huge, hard hands. I eat and watch them covertly. They are silent for the most part, exchanging short grunts of conversation about the weather or the job in hand.

I finish drinking my coffee and check my watch. Le Grand is now well into his flight. I imagine him, far above me, like some kind of business-class angel. He is probably sleeping. I picture him in one of those first class seat-beds, an elegant air hostess refilling his champagne glass. Right. Everything is set up, so I'll run out to call Debs. She sounded really off last night. A quick little chat might set it all right. But when I call her, the phone rings out. I imagine I can hear it trill shrilly around our house. Where is she? I wonder. Since she was laid off, she's nearly always at home, watching TV in the living room. Sometimes I come home from work and she's lying on the sofa, and I just know she's barely moved all day. Maybe she's out looking for work? *Good on you, Debs*, I think resolutely, though I know it's much more likely she's gone to the shop to refill her teabag and Jaffa cake supplies.

Time has never gone so slowly. I shower and change, trying to draw out the time. The tiny bathroom is almost unbelievably uncomfortable. Trying to manoeuvre around it is like playing an elaborate game of Tetris. When I try and get out of the shower, I am jammed tight between the lavatory and the basin. When I'm sitting down on the lavatory, the toilet roll holder digs painfully into my hip. Once I'm ready (one careful hair-combing later). I flick on the small, blurred TV and try to stay in Room 206 for an hour or so, but the seconds crawl by terribly slowly in the confined space. Instead I get up and go downstairs, where I pace about in the lobby, thankful for the relative expanse of carpet to walk about on. I queue dutifully for the business computer and log on to my email. Nothing exciting. John from Accounts wonders if I have submitted my expenses for my trip to Dublin. I shrug. John can wait till I get home and check. I check my Facebook. I fill in my status update – Rich *is off in London, waiting for a client to fly in from Canada.* There, that looks impressive. I check Debs' status. It's an odd one. She's written Debs *is waiting for something to happen.* I message her cheerily – 'Something good will happen!' but even though the green spot beside her name says she is online, she doesn't reply.

I pace around a little more. He should be landing now. *'Thank you so much for coming here today. We know you will be as excited about this possibility as we are.'* I walk through his journey in my head. Taxi from Heathrow, I guess. No bus or Tube journeys for Le Grand. Slowly the time ticks by.

'Nearly ready to go now, sir?' asks the kind, older man behind the desk. I feel a sudden, absurd desire to ask him to come to the presentation, but instead, take the lift up to the conference room. There I straighten the tablecloth and angle the projector a tiny bit to the right. Perfect. I wonder about coffee. Should I order it now? I check my watch. He should be here any minute. I decide to wait, and ask him what he wants.

Half an hour later, I am sweating in my suit. No sign of Le Grand. My mouth feels like it contains too much saliva. I check at the front desk.

'No sir, no messages.' What do I do now? I queue up for the business computer and wait, agitatedly for a woman to finish typing a slow email. No emails. No messages. I walk up and down the foyer. Did he get the directions to the hotel wrong? Did he change his mind? Is he coming at all? And even more frightening – *did something I say put him off coming?* I have sweated through my shirt, I feel it cling, limp and cold on my back. *Please let him come*, I think. *Please don't let me lose my job.*

Somehow the afternoon passes. I check the Canadian flight on the internet. It seems to have landed on time. Perhaps he missed it? Perhaps he is getting the next one? I don't dare leave my spot in the foyer to run down and ring Michael. I compromise instead and settle on emailing him. I am conflicted. Should I tell him just how much I'm afraid he's not coming? Am I over-reacting? The last thing I want to do is for Michael to think of me as naïve and jumpy. In the end I simply tell him Le Grand seems to be delayed, and that I am going to wait until I hear from him. I also send Michael my phone number here.

Another hour passes. Michael doesn't ring. I have two jittery cups of coffee, courtesy of the reception staff, who have taken pity on me. Ragesh is the older one, gently-spoken, compassionate.

'I see this all the time, sir,' he says. 'Flights delayed, flights missed.'

I check my mail intermittently. Finally, a mail from Michael. *Le Grand's people have got in touch. His meetings ran on in Toronto. He's getting the next flight out, but he won't arrive till tomorrow. Same time. Just ask the staff there to extend your booking, and Janine here will change your flight. It'll be worth it to get that meeting. Michael.* Short and to the point. I feel a sense of relief, of respite.

'Hey Ragesh!' I call, 'You're right. He was delayed.' I am smiling broadly. I decide then to change out of my suit and go for a walk. The air feels cool and welcoming on my face. Right, what now? Phone calls, I suppose, and then dinner. I stop by the phone booth, and punch out Michael's mobile number.

'Yes?'

'I got your message,' I tell him. 'Is he definitely confirmed tomorrow?'

'Yes'. There is a banging noise in the background, a raised voice. 'Sorry, Rich, bit busy here. All OK your end? Hotel fine?'

'Great!' I say with idiotic enthusiasm. 'Couldn't be better.'

'Good man. See you when you're back.' There is a click on the line. He is gone. I sigh and start to press out my home number. Again, the phone rings. I fancy I can hear it echo through darkened rooms. *Where are you?* I wonder. I try her mobile. It rings a few times. I am just about to put it down when she answers.

'Rich?'

'Deborah! Finally! Where have you been?' There is a silence, and then she says, 'I'm just here at home.'

'At home? I just called there. It rang out.'

'We're having trouble with the phone line,' she says. 'Bloody phone company.' Her voice is quick and uneven. Is she upset? I try to change the subject. 'Any news?'

'What news would there be? Aren't you meant to be with what-his-name?'

'He's delayed, not arriving till tomorrow.' I remember to add. 'I'll be another day, is that OK?'

'Of course!' Her response surprises me. 'If it's your job you have to. Anyway, it's no hardship being stuck in London, is it?'

I look out of the phone box. A woman with a deadened face walks by, limping slightly in her heels. There is a tramp urinating with his back to me. A dirty newspaper takes flight down the street and plasters itself to the glass of the phone box. 'Sure,' I say lightly. 'Lucky me.'

I buy a kebab and a bottle of beer and go back to the tiny room I now know as well as my own face.

The next morning is riddled with déjà vu. I get up, have breakfast with the same builders, wrangle a wash in the tiny bathroom, and by noon I am back in the lobby again. I debate about staying in my room, but the walls are starting to remind me of the Star Wars trash compactor. The earliest Le Grand can arrive is at two pm, so that still gives me a few hours. I stroll down the street. It is starting to mist rain, droplets lightly stinging my face. I wander in and out of shops around Earl's Court, admiring the smartly dressed hordes on the pavement, and treat myself to a leisurely latte in the nearby Starbucks.

Thank you so much for coming here today. We know you will be as excited about this possibility as we are. I am much more relaxed than yesterday. I feel strangely at home in this shabby hotel and its neighbourhood. In my head I have mapped the area; now I know the route to the phone box, to the shop, to the Tube, to the off-license, to the Lebanese restaurant. I smile at Ragesh as I check the time. Almost two o'clock. Just enough time to check my mails.

I flip through my inbox, spam, spam, boring work email, nothing of interest. I check Facebook out of idle habit. Friends are having a party tomorrow night – I must try and make it if I fly back on time. Then I see Deborah's status. I read it again. Then I read the comments underneath. All the air has left my body. Deborah *is moving on with her life.* Underneath her best friend Leanne has written 'What about Rich?' The most devastating thing is Debs' simple reply. 'It's complicated'. *No, it's not!* I think, breathless with shock. *It's very simple. We're married.* I look at those hateful words again and again. No use. I need to talk to her.

In the phone box, I misdial her number twice. My hands are shaking.

'Debs?' *Thank God, thank God, finally there.*

'Rich.' Her voice is flat, unfriendly.

'Debs, Deborah, I just checked Facebook. What on earth do you mean by writing you are "moving on"?'

There is a long sigh. 'Because I am. Because I've wanted to for a long time.' I am silent. Blood thuds in my ears. 'Rich, you must have known. You had to have known. It's been awful. All those fights. Since you left the other day I've been thinking and, well, I'm moving out.'

I clutch the shelf of the phone box for support. 'Moving out? Listen, we need to talk, as soon as I have this meeting over, I'll come home. I'll ask Janine to change my flight to tonight. Please!'

Her voice doesn't even sound angry, or upset, just cold and determined. 'No. there's no point.' Behind her I can hear a man's voice.

'Is someone there with you?'

She sighs again. 'You might as well know. It's Michael. Michael you work with.'

I hang up, go outside and sit down heavily on the pavement. *This can't just have happened. It can't. Deborah. With Michael? With my boss?* I wipe my sweaty forehead on my clean shirt cuff. I think, idiotically, in the words of the song – *How long has this been going on?*

I am so angry and upset; my thoughts are zigzags, bursts of emotion, sudden revelations. *Was Michael trying to get me out of the country? Is this why I'm here? Is there even a Le Grand?* I want to throw back my head and howl like a beast. But some small part of me realises that I can't do this. Not in the afternoon, in Earl's Court. Instead I execute a classic stumble into the nearest bar.

Two drinks later, I am calming down. *I will go home and talk to her, I think. It might just be a one-off, a blip. After all, it's been seven years. That counts.* The pub smells dank, with a sharp undertone of ammonia. The only other drinkers are two old men, bleary with pints, mouths moving slowly as they tell long stories to each other. I shake myself. Time to go. Collect my stuff. Head off. My eyes are throbbing. My throat hurts.

'Oh, Mr. Brown! Mr. Le Grand was here an hour ago, sir,' says the polite Ragesh. His face is worried. 'He was asking for you, sir. He waited until ten minutes ago, and then left.'

I run down the steps outside the hotel. The rain is coming down, in heavy, warm blotches that stipple the pavement and spot my clothes. I am flooded with pure, pure panic. I grab the arm of a man in a suit passing by.

'Are you Le Grand?' I demand. He shakes his head. I turn and grab another man's sleeve. 'Are you Le Grand?' He doesn't respond, but brushes off my arm and walks away, faster. 'Are you?' I shout at the newspaper vendor across the street. 'Are you?'

He doesn't answer. Just in case he is – just in case there *is* a Le Grand – I brush away the tears on my face, smooth down my dirty, damp suit and say loudly and with dignity. 'Thank you so much for coming here today. We know you will be as excited about this possibility as we are…'

SEALED

It is morning. The sun dapples through the window-pane, making little pools of warmth on my bedspread. I lie snug, safe, my duvet wrapped tight around me, and dance my fingers in and out of the patches of shadow and light. I hear the front door slam, the engine cough, splutter, catch. When I close my eyes, I can picture the blue truck kick up dust puffs in the hard, rutted tracks. He is gone for the day.

I don't know if I love it or hate it when he is gone.

I get up slowly. There is no rush, no rush at all. I move carefully to the kitchen, one step at a time, down the corridor, hands brushing both walls in a delicate trail from room to room. I flick the switch of the kettle, on, off, on, off, on, off, on. I hum the Pixies' song under my breath – 'If man is five/then the Devil is six/and God is seven'. Three is good too, magical, but seven is the number I need today. Everything needs to go well.

My breakfast is always the same. I like ritual. I choose a striped white and brown mug and a white plate decorated with brown discs. My toast pops out and I butter it, carefully cutting off the crusts in a symmetrical manner. I can feel the nervousness in my shaking hand as I lift the slice to my mouth, in my throat muscles that convulse around the toast. Even my teeth seem to ache root-deep as I bite in.

I clear away the plate and cup, rinse and stack precisely. Slowly I do the warm up exercises my body still remembers. Bend, Twist. Stretch. *I can do it* I think, over and over. *I can walk. I can fly. I can do it.*

When I open the kitchen door, I feel my legs grow heavier. The glass pane at the top of the door puddles light on the floor, a dazzling, greenish glow, a light of trees and grass and summer outside. I step into the hall. Seven tiles. I stand precisely in the centre of the first tile. It is cool under my bare feet. One step. Two. I am sweating now. Great gouts of perspiration soak my armpits, my back, my top lip. Three. Four. My breath trembles in my chest, rasping in, out, awkwardly, as if I have forgotten how to inhale and exhale. Five. Six. *Just one more* I think, *I can walk. I can fly. I can do it.*

But I can't. My legs stop moving. I am frozen, the seventh step lying before me, a foot of floor. It might as well be a wall. I slide slowly down, and come to rest in a slumped position. I am heavy as lead, limbs useless and slack.

Once I was a dancer. I spun and drifted like a feather under the burning lights of the stage, exposed to the endless, white circle-faces melting into darkness. I danced and thought only of the music, the position of my arms and legs, the beautiful symphony of my body as it moved, sure and confident on the sprung, wooden floor.

I am still lying in the corridor when he comes home that evening. 'My God!' He strides by me, his walk bristling with anger. His face is closed with contempt. The kitchen door shuts. 'My God!' His voice rises from behind the door, clear and hard. 'You've been lying round all day! There's no food! The place is filthy!' I raise my head. He is back in the hallway. He looks at me for the first time in a long time, and his eyes are ugly with rage. 'You really are useless,' he says softly, and shuts the door.

At least he never touches me. He is too repulsed. I think I would go mad if he did.

It is a week later. I wait in bed till he is gone. The sounds of the truck die away and my small world returns to a fragile peace. Today is not a day for thinking about going. I make my bed, folding the covers tight as a cocoon, I dust the bedside table. I polish the mirror. There is a small rush of relief that comes when I do these things, a tiny easement. The ball of anxiety retreats a little further down my throat.

My world is small but I have become an expert in its details. Its limits are the walls – see, I touch them, one by one, round and round the house I go. Inside I am safe. I keep to the rituals. I don't think about his voice – *lalalalalalala*, I sing inside my head. I don't think about his face. Instead I am a brittle, careful automaton, a cleaning robot. All of my movements are slow and cautious, calculated. I clean the cooker, I scrub the floor, I defrost pork chops and I wipe down the counters. I wash the bathroom floor and scour out the bath and toilet till they sparkle with a bluish-white porcelain glow. I clean everywhere, all but his bedroom, where I am not meant to disturb. I imagine it as a festering dull room, curtains pulled, mounds of clothes all reeking with his ugly scent. I picture my feet replaced by wheels, my hands by metal hooks, antiseptic, gleaming. And round and round I go. Round and round like a little ticking clockwork mouse until he returns home.

He's in a better mood tonight. I see his dark gaze run around the kitchen, his face relaxing as he smells the rosemary scent of the cooking meat. 'Better,' he says, sitting down the pulling off his work boots. They lie, dirty and careless on my polished floor. I feel an uncontrollable urge to pick them up and hide them away, but I know it will annoy him. So I serve the dinner on the beautifully laid table and try not to look at them. *Lalalalalalala. I will not look at them.* I pour his beer. *I will not look at them.* My face is prickling with an itch, *I can do it. I will not look at them.*

I am sweating behind my eyes now. 'What's wrong with you?' His voice is disgusted. I can't take it, I run and grab the boots, and scuttle down the hall to the cupboard, where they are *meant* to be. I will worry about their dirtiness later. 'Come back here!' he yells. 'Sit down like a human being, for God's sake!' I walk back slowly, warily. 'Sit down. Eat.' I obey, but the mood has changed. He has remembered that I am broken, useless. I sit down with eyes lowered, but that only makes him angrier. He slaps his hands on the table. 'Eat. Don't sulk.' he roars. He grabs my shoulder. 'Just like your mother,' he says. His breath is hot and poisonous on my face.

Later, I lie in the darkness and think of her. I don't think of the last time, the chill of the floor, the hard, cool surface of her face, her eyelashes painted on her cheeks like a perfect ink-drawing. I remember instead the warm, powdery smell of the skin in the crook between her neck and shoulder, and how I nestled my face there when she hugged me. I see her face crease in a quick grin, the tiny, endless movements on her hands when she sewed, a flowing stream of embroidered panels, and more mundane things, sheets, pillowcases, and – of course – my breath hitches as I remember – my dance costumes. How she loved them! I remember the soft drift of the tutus as they settled around her knees, the flash of colour as she worked on the intricate appliques of the leotards. How she loved the fact that I was a dancer! A small sob builds large in my throat, so it swells and hurts with the contained pain of her.

It was all so sudden, you see.

I always knew that there was a strangeness about my home. There was no father there, for one thing. I still have some vague memories of a dark man, and shouting voices, but that's it. My mother *was* the home. Her bright presence filled it, like the yellow radiance of a lamp. Everywhere were traces of her, her embroidery, her beautifully polished pots and her books. It was a nest house, and I loved it. So did she, so much so that she never left it.

'Why do I need to go out?' she would ask me, when I whined and plagued her to come with me on one of my planned expeditions; to the fair, the circus, the beach. 'Won't you enjoy it more with your friends?' All of our groceries were delivered, as well as the wools and threads and heavy book packages. We were self-contained and sealed, and apart from my daily to and fro to school (a mere three streets away) and occasional expeditions with school-friends, I was happy to stay inside, in our own little world. She would stroke my hair and tell me stories, and I would doze against her as we sat on the sofa, snug in the warm, flickering light of the TV.

And then it all changed.

She was so proud at first, of my dancing. She would get me to practice my steps, dressed in the costumes her deft, quick hands had made. 'Beautiful,' she would breathe, watching me, her eyes soft and alight, as I spun, quick, quicker, quickest on the expanse of kitchen floor. She listened to all my stories of rivalries, successes, failures, hopes, with all the gravity that a fourteen year old could hope for. And at first that was all I needed.

But as the year rolled on, I improved, I got bigger and bigger roles; finally I came home one day incandescent with excitement. I was dancing the role of The Sugar Plum Fairy in an excerpt from the Nutcracker at the school Christmas concert. As usual, she gently refused my invitation. I became more insistent. I desperately wanted her to come and see me dance.

'Why won't you come and see me? All the other mothers do!' I raged and stormed around the house, and even when she tried to placate me with pancakes, a new skirt, I remained cold and angry. I carried on my dense, black sulk for the whole week. Every time I was at home I would avoid her; when she came into a room I would pointedly move from it. I was determined to break her stupid resolve to stay at home.

When I remember it now, her soft, anguished face, her endless attempts to bribe me with food and treats, I feel stomach-sick, my heart like a lead bucket falling endlessly inside me. I cry in the darkness, quiet, soaking tears that pool damp on my pillow.

The next day I try again. I get out of the kitchen. I get into the hall. Over the next hour I step, carefully and exactly, tile by tile – one, two, three, four and five. Then I stop, and as much as I want to, as much as I try, I can't make myself move any further towards the door. My body, once a weapon of agility and power, has failed me again. I sit on the cold tiled floor and cry.

I was dancing on stage when he came. I spun and drifted like a feather under the burning lights of the stage, exposed to the endless, white circle-faces melting into darkness. I danced and thought only of the music, the position of my arms and legs, the beautiful symphony of my body as it moved, sure and confident on the sprung, wooden floor. I am wearing a tiara and gauzy wings, pale pink and almost transparent. I know I am beautiful. I dance and it is perfection, joy, I am strong and fearless and powerful. I could dance forever.

Out of the corner of my eye, I see a commotion backstage. A heavy-set man is arguing with the music teacher. I see her hands clap over her mouth in horror, as she turns to the stage. The piano-playing stops abruptly. *What?* The curtains are jerking shut, across a vista of confused faces. I pause, arm still extended upwards, feet pointed out, frozen in the correct fourth position. When all the faces turn to me, I know it is bad. I am stone-still. I want to know. I never want to know. I must know. The big man pushes past them. He has a uniform, and his face is sad and crumpled, like a Shar-Pei dog. I find I can move my hands, I use them to push him back, to stop him saying it. But he does. 'It's your mother,' he says quietly. That is all I dreaded hearing. Like a paper bag I fold in on myself. I fall, weightless, hollow.

She had been trying to leave the house. To watch me dance, just like I'd demanded. She was at the gate when a car spun around on the ice, and crashed, taking her with it; in one cruel, black-scratched skid, she went and with her went everything. In the long, black, senseless days afterwards, he came and took me. My father's brother. My uncle. A large dark man, with a large, dark, scowling face, he was the only living relative I seemed to have. I went from the little glowing cottage to this soulless house.

Why did I try to make her leave the house? I cannot change this brutal fact, but I can atone for it. This house is my prison, my warder that dark man I do not call uncle. Every corner of my cell has been memorized, every line of his hated face, his hair, greying now, his cold blue eyes. I will serve my time, repentant, in this house of gloom. Since I've come here, I try and preserve her through my memories, the few photos I have. It has been so long since I saw her that I feel a breathless ache under my ribs. I need her here so much, but every night, her image gets fainter, her face, when I can remember it, is the face from that last row, her frightened, placatory face. I lie in the darkness, my throat burning with tears. Every day, I think of her. When I look in the mirror I try to see her in my eyes, my expressions. I am a poor copy, an inaccurate replica. My body mimics her cleaning rituals. It mimics everything I can remember about her.

I am now her only mirror in this world.

#

Summer turns to autumn. I see the green-glow of leaves outside replaced by a papery, flaking carpet of orange and brown. The skies turn grey, weeping with a dull horizontal rain that sleets sideways across the windows. His temper gets worse. The truck takes longer and longer to start in the cold mornings. I lie in bed and listen as it coughs and retches its way to life. The dying buzz of its engine is my cue to get up and start my busy-work. One day I take everything out of the cupboards and scour the shelves. On another I wax the furniture, like my mother showed me, carefully rubbing in the beeswax to the wood till it shines with a rosy lustre. *Tick tock, tick-tock.* My body is clockwork, my movements an endless series of perfect repetitions. With each ritual I am counting off the endless minutes of my sentence. I dust between the banisters, delicately removing little cobwebs, powdery dust.

The first time I tried leaving was the worst. It was just a few days after I'd come here, to this dull, chill house, and I couldn't bear it anymore. My hatred felt like a physical pulse in my stomach – the long silences, his surly voice, his open resentment of my presence, all festered together in an ugly lump. I had decided. I was going to run away, back to my old village, and beg someone, anyone I trusted, to take me in. I didn't know where he had put my mother's possessions, so I just packed a few things – money, a bus timetable, change of clothes, a book. I made it as far as the hallway before my vision started to fog with dizziness. As I stepped forward, the walls seemed to spin, the black and white tiles started to buckle and recede under my feet. I started to shake, stomach-sick, and stopped. I remember thinking *Maybe it's easier if I crawl?* That got me a few feet further, eyes closed, flat to the floor, worming my way forward. I even got a hand on the slick painted wood of the door. But I couldn't do it. I couldn't make the final step. I just crawled over to the wall and lay there, shaking and sick, till I managed to stumble back to my room.

Since then I've tried to leave so many times. Each failure weighs me down, more and more, until all I want to do is lie in bed and ache, swollen with unshed tears.

#

The days get colder. I watch the ice-patterns melt on the windows, magical, silvered ferns painted on the panes. It is my birthday today. No-one knows. I haven't been at school in almost a year now. I trace an absent finger over the leaf patterns. The truck is gone. The house has the tinny echo of emptiness. I look around the kitchen. It is spotless. I feel a curious disinclination to clean today. I feel something – annoyance? Upset? No, *dissatisfaction*, I think, pleased at having identified it so accurately. The day wears on. I try to get back to my cleaning schedule, but nothing alleviates the tension today. I drift from room to room, looking but not seeing, moving and replacing objects. Outside the light changes slowly from the hard bright brilliance of winter sunshine to the grey gloom of twilight. It is dark inside and outside when I finally sit down. The clock ticks loudly on the wall. Six thirty. He is normally home by six. I am restless. I don't like changes to my routine. Six forty-five. Seven. My fingers tap on the polished work surface. Seven fifteen. Abruptly the phone shrills beside me, an angry, drilling sound. I jump and stare. It is one of the first times I have ever heard it ring. *Brrrrrr-ing!* The sharp sound echoes again, hard against the walls. I grab the cold plastic receiver.

'Hello. Who is this?' My voice is hushed as if he can hear.

There is a long sigh. 'It's me, you stupid girl.' Him. My heart starts to beat faster, like a little tap-hammer in my chest. He clears his throat noisily. 'Fuckin' truck's broken down. I'll be home tomorrow.' His voice drops. 'Don't do anything stupid.' There is a silence broken by the crackle of the line, and faint traffic noises in the background. I picture him, angry and abandoned, on a roadside phone, several towns away. The blackness lifts in my chest. 'Yes,' I say, and hang up.

It is freedom, of a sort. I am temporarily mistress of this dark house. I can shout if I want to. I can eat whatever I want. I wander restlessly up and down the corridor. I can watch television! The only TV set is in his room. I hear it at night, tinny echoes of canned laughter echoing through the house. I am entranced, briefly, at the thought if being able to watch bright, normal, TV lives. There is all night to watch it, and all morning to let the set cool down. He will never know I've been in there.

I push open the door. It is not at all as I pictured it. There is slight unpleasant smell, of soured breath and closed windows. But the room is strangely tidy. I look around. The bed is made. The wardrobe door is closed neatly on its contents. A chair is heaped with folded shirts, but they seem clean. I sit gingerly on the edge of the bed. I put on the TV. It roars to life, with a sharp bark of static, and then settles into the nine o'clock news. I watch, fascinated by the mundane details, the presenter's immaculate blonde hair, the shots of idyllic countryside accompanying a story. My gaze strays around the room. I am fascinated by this forbidden room, and how disappointingly bland it is. Bed, chair, wardrobe, framed family photograph, and – *wait!* – my breath flutters in my chest. I clutch my throat. There is a box in the corner. A large wooden box that I recognise.

My hands are like ice as I fumble at the catch. As long as I remember, this box has stood in the corner of my living room at home. It was our important document box, the one that we stored my birth-cert in, my school reports, our insurance documents. It finally swings open and I delve in, with hungry, desperate grabs. There are so many documents, piled to the top. I take them out, one by one, and fan them out on the floor. There is a pile of official documents that I don't bother to read. There are photos. So many photos of me, as a baby, a child, photos of me in my dance costumes. I keep sifting through the box. My breath catches! It is a photo of my mother. Her face is alight and smiling. It was Christmas, I remember. Her lap is covered in the silly little gifts I bought her. My eyes burn and itch with hot, unshed tears.

There is a wrapped package. I open it. Inside is my fairy costume. I briefly wonder how it came to rest here. I remember wearing it home that day. I remember standing in it, my thin ballet shoes wet and cold, my feet numbed as I stood, silent and terrified at the gate, the streak of red across the slush. I remember the policeman's hand on my shoulder, warm and heavy, the only still point in a world of pain and snow.

I am crying openly now as I rummage through the box. More photos fall like confetti from my hands. I see my life drop onto the floor; my confident, happy face smiles out at me. More documents. More photos. And under it all, a grubby, marked collection of letters. I pull them out and read them slowly. Then again, until it is dark. I switch on the lamp. Then I read them again.

My face is wet, but I don't even notice. The letters are wonderful. They are from my mother's sister, the first from around the time of my birth, judging by the dates, the last from just before – *just before the accident*, I finish firmly in my mind. My aunt writes to my mother, and I can almost hear her gentle voice as I read the words.

She is as beautiful as you say. She makes me wish I had a child of my own. I see so much of you reflected in her – the eyes, the smile.

She writes about their shared condition. *Do you think it's because of what happened when we were children? I blame Mum for locking us away. We didn't get to leave the house for so long. I wish it hadn't recurred. I want to see you.*

And over and over again. *I wish I could meet my niece.*

I sit there all night, in the darkness, holding the letters, until the sun comes up. It is a beautiful winter morning. The sun dazzles against the window-panes.

It is time.

I am numb. I cannot think; thinking will stop me, block me. My movements are automatic. I put on the fairy costume, struggling to clasp the gauzy wings into place. It is tight, but not too tight. I push open the door. The light is white-bright. It hits my eyes like a hard hammer-stroke.

I step outside.

I am wild, I am alive, I am a fish swimming in the breathless, cold, intoxicating air. The gate, path, trees are brighter and bigger than I ever dreamt of. The world whirls around me, but it is no longer the sick-spin of nausea, but a glorious swirl of light and colour – *The smells! The sounds!* And finally, triumphantly *I can do it. I can walk. I can do it. I can fly.*

A LOVELY PLACE TO LIVE

It's a very pretty estate, small and green and uniform, with rows of obedient red-brick houses and perfectly trimmed trees. The prettiest street of all is the cul-de-sac right at the end. In springtime the cherry tree on the lawn of No. 4 explodes like a soft-petalled vision in baby-pink. In summer time, the estate hums with lawnmowers and blazes with a window-box symphony of yellows, purples, reds. In autumn the lawns are demarcated by neat brown piles of leaves, and in winter the paths are sensibly salted and ice-free. I'd love to tell you where it is, but I don't think the others would like that. It's not the kind of estate that wants visitors, you see. I think you can picture it. It's an elegant middle-class suburb on the outskirts of a large Irish town. Let's leave it like that.

I wander across it while house-hunting, and am immediately enchanted. 'A cul-de-sac with only five houses. Ideal. It's so…quiet…' The estate agent smiles at me with red plastic lips. 'Yes, it is,' she agrees. 'And we want to keep it that way.'

We? I look at her. 'Oh, I live a few streets down, my dear. It's really a lovely place to live. Quiet, nice neighbours, near the town, but not too near.' I wander out of the kitchen and into the downstairs sitting room. It's clean, airy, bright, with lots of space for my desk and my bookshelves. 'I'll take it,' I say decisively.

Her hands flutter in a jerky motion. 'Oh, lovely. Though of course we will need to check your references.' She consults her clipboard. 'You work at a school? Teaching art?' I nod. 'For my sins.' I laugh, but she doesn't. 'I'm actually a writer in my spare time.'

'O-ooooh.' She manages to draw the word out into an elongated syllable. Her lips pucker, lemon-sour. 'But you're a full-time teacher?' The word 'teacher' seems to reassure her. 'Oh, I am indeed. Permanent and pensionable.' She visibly relaxes. 'Then just the references, dear, I'm sure they'll be fine. But you can never be too careful.'

Well, my references must have gone through successfully;

Sean the headmaster mentions to me that he'd provided one. Well, what he actually says is, 'Some crazy woman called me up and wanted to know every detail of your life. So many questions!' He shakes his head, harassed at the memory. 'So I just told her you were an angel in human form. That seemed to satisfy her.' And so it does. Precisely one week later I am helping the removal men lug my boxes off the van and into my neat little house. I can see some of my new neighbours watching from the row of five little houses. I wave cheerily at them. One teenage boy waves back enthusiastically and keeps waving, until his mother pulls his arm down sharply. The others nod in a slightly embarrassed fashion and keep at their various chores, one man and his dog setting off for a walk, the mother watering the herbaceous border as her son rakes the grass. Across the wall I can see the heads of children appear and disappear as they bounce on an invisible trampoline, their clear, high squawks carrying on the still air. Half an hour later, when the last of the boxes is sliding off the van-flap into my arms, I hear a man clear his throat behind me.

'Welcome to the street,' he says. He is a large, solid man wearing a suit and a pink shirt. His bluff red face is creased in a smile. I slide the box back in and take his extended hand, pulling a wry face. 'Sorry about the state of dishevelment – filthy business, moving house.'

'Not at all, not at all,' he says loudly. 'I'm John, and I live next door. If you need anything, just ask myself or the wife, Maureen.' I've seen Maureen already, a pale ghost peeping out her downstairs window.

'Thanks John.' I am tickled by his officious welcome. My last apartment was in the city centre, where I shared a third floor with some students, a Latvian porter and two young policemen. I had no idea what their names were, and even now they probably didn't realise that I'd moved.

'It's nice here,' he says, nodding. 'We try to keep it looking good. No drop in property prices here!' He laughs heartily.

'Good job I didn't buy the house, so,' I say, forcing a smile on my face.

'Ah well, it's nice to have you on the street. Take care now.' He is already moving away. I am carrying in the last box when I turn and see him inspecting the grass verge. The van is too wide for the drive, and the right tyres have churned up a broken seam of mud and grass. He draws his face up into a frown and shakes his head slowly, side to side. I bite my lip, shift the box onto my hip, then keep walking in to the house. *Fussy old eejit!* I think. I am dusty and cross.

John's not too bad, I soon decide. He's fussy, alright, head of the Residents Committee, a member of the Neighbourhood Watch and a veritable pillar of the local community. But there are benefits to his control-freakery. The street is impeccable. Noise levels are gentle. His cowed wife spends most of her days cleaning. In the late afternoons, through our adjoining wall, I can hear the dim hum of the hoover interspersed with bursts of TV soaps. She sometimes gives me a shy wave. The path of grass between our houses is immaculate; I imagine her cutting it with nail-scissors, pin-precise. She weeds my lawn, I'm almost sure. Sometimes I suspect she even polishes my bins – well, they stay shiny, with no attention from me. The house next to me is for sale, a red sign mounted in the front garden. People come to view the house. I watch the estate agent who showed me my own house usher them around. We wave at each other. In the next house down the street is a nervous older lady called Susan, who lives with her son Tony. Tony is about fifteen but doesn't go to school. He has a marvellous, slow smile that he directs at everyone he meets, and a bike that he rides slowly round and round the estate in great, looping curves. In the next house is a small but energetic family, a man, a woman, a child, a dog, all of them in a state of perpetual motion. As I sit in front of my desk I see them pass by the window, the woman and child walking the dog, the man on his bike, the man returning on his bike and jogging back to meet the others. Up and down the cul-de-sac they go, never stopping, travelling in different combinations, the woman holding the dog-lead, the child aloft on his father's shoulders, the dog leaping alongside.

Everyone knows who I am. Even the postman knows who I am, and takes great pleasure in telling me. 'You're the teacher,' he tells me. 'The new lassie on the street.' He thumbs deliberately through his satchel. 'You're in the school out by the lake.' They are not questions, but I nod.

He smiles, pleased, and abandons the pretence of looking for my post.

Time ticks by, all is quiet, predictable, serene. The days darken. The leaves on the cherry tree turn brown and drift onto the grass. I wake up one morning and they are gone. I learn. I start raking my leaves. Hallowe'en. I hear the sounds of children whooping and calling on the streets nearby. My bowl of sweets stands by the door, but no-one calls. I nod. *It's not that kind of street.* There are no plastic skeletons in evidence anywhere in the cul-de-sac, no pumpkins, no mock cobwebs. (There were some real cobwebs stretching round my door, but I suspect Maureen's twitching J-cloth exorcised both them and their creators). It gets colder. The street smells of log fires and frost. We call in mock-chagrin to each other in the mornings as we scrape our windshields. Christmas comes and goes, neat little trees twinkle in windows up and down the street. The days begin to lengthen into pearly grey evenings. All is clockwork-perfect, right up until my heart attack.

Cardiac incident, the nurses say, but the evasiveness of that term annoys me. I wake up one night, with a mild but persistent pain in my chest. Rolling over I try to get comfortable, but my heart starts to quicken. A little pulse drums in my ear. I draw in a deep breath, but there is a rubber band tightening over my chest. The pain gets a little sharper. I realise I am now fully awake and registering my symptoms. *Surely not. I'm young.* The feeling of disbelief persists as I hold on to the bedpost and dial the emergency services. I feel indignant, scared, breathless. My breath is starting to crush in my lungs but I force myself out of my ratty cotton pyjamas and into some fresh blue satin ones. Halfway into the pyjama trousers I have to sit down and rest before dragging the other leg in. I hear the doorbell go, and inch my way down the stairs. 'It's probably nothing…' I say faintly as my water-weak legs give out and I sit down heavily on the floor. Between the legs of the ambulance men, I glimpse Susan on my lawn in her dressing gown, her mouth a dark O of distress.

When I come home, my sister Leigh comes to stay for a week. She is impressed with the snow of cards that has fallen inside the letterbox. 'That damn postman,' I say faintly.

'I bet he's told everyone.' I have been told to rest, to eat healthily, and then to do a little mild exercise. The computer is out of bounds; instead I lie swaddled on the sofa. Leigh is patient but I am a bad patient. I sulk and fret. I cry quietly under my blanket. I resent my new limitations. Neighbours pass by my windows. Sometimes they wave at me. Susan accosts Leigh in the local shop. Leigh recounts the meeting to me later with gusto. 'She pulled at my sleeve – no, *really*, she actually did that – and said in a shaky voice "You're her sister, aren't you. I've seen you go in and out. Tell her I'm praying for her."' Leigh is scornful. I am touched.

Leigh leaves to go back to her family. 'If I don't go now, they'll have the house burned down' she says resignedly and gives me a tight hug. The next time Susan wanders slowly by, I open the door. She won't come in, but fidgets nervously on the doorstep. 'Can I get you anything?' she asks. 'I'm fine,' I say warmly. 'Thanks for the card.' She shakes her head. 'It's nothing.' There is a pause, then suddenly she grabs my arm, quick and birdlike. 'Thank God you're all right. We're all so relieved.'

To my surprise they really *are*. Even John and Maureen come for an official visit. I see his eyes flick approvingly over the surfaces Leigh has meticulously cleaned before leaving, despite my protestations. 'Just because you are a slob doesn't mean I have to live in filth,' she'd said cheerily, flicking me with the dustpan.

'Well, now, you gave us all a fright there,' he pronounces as he gravely eats a chocolate biscuit. I am not allowed chocolate biscuits.

'Ah, I'm fine now.' I don't like to dwell on it. 'The bit of time off work is doing me the world of good.'

'Still and all,' he continues – you can't interrupt John when he's in full flow – 'you might need a bit of helping out for the next while. Susan's lad will take out your bins.' I bow my head in assent. 'Tom will do your lawn.' *Tom*? I think, confused, *oh, Hyperactive Man, of course, that's his name.* I nod again.

'Any news from the estate?' I am grateful but resentful of the need for help.

'Well.' He dunks his biscuit and stirs it around. A chocolate slick swirls in the tea. 'The good news is that I keep checking the value of the property for sale next door, and it's consistent. God help those in negative equity, that's what I say. The bad news is, at the last residents' committee meeting, I heard there was a bit of trouble at the lower end of the estate.' The lower end of the estate is near the corner shop, where teenage kids cluster in the evenings, drawn like track-suited moths to the glow from the shop window. It is our middle-class ghetto. Some of the lawns are untidy. The children scream a little louder there. One man washes his car, shirtless, every Sunday.

'Really?'

'Oh yes. There's been a couple of lads sighted. You know, hanging round with cans of drink, shouting. Mrs. Dolan saw them looking over her back wall. Out for what they can rob, I'd say.' He looks out my window. 'Actually, I was going to ask you something. Seeing as you're a bit laid up here, could you keep an eye out for us on this road?' Maureen makes a noise, as if to speak, then sits back and lifts her cup to her pale lips. I am not offended.

'Like *Rear Window*?' I ask mischievously.

He laughs and slaps his leg. 'The very same! Good woman! Now just keep a look out. Maureen here is doing her bit.' Maureen nods on cue, obediently. 'I don't want to ask Susan though, that poor woman has enough to do with her son, and Tom's family are too busy.'

'No problem, John.' I say, a little faintly. I see myself being sucked into the suburban hierarchy of the Neighbourhood Watch.

Actually it's quite engrossing. Lying on the sofa, I see things I've missed before. Tom's brown Labrador dog gets walked four times a day, usually by Tom himself. No lie. He is an old dog, and by the third or fourth call, he no longer jumps up; instead he climbs to his feet like a weary old man and plods off, head wagging slightly. Susan's son Tony trundles my bin down the gravel drive to the corner, the wheels biting into the crunchy surface. Maureen has started polishing my windows. It is very kind of her, but somewhat distracting. It is impossible to callously watch TV while she slaves, squeaking her cloth over the panes, so I end up perching outside on the wooden bench to talk to her while she labours. She is disturbed by my attempts to socialise.

'Oh no,' she says in a soft, distressed voice. 'You'll be cold.' It is cold, but I have a large tartan blanket around my shoulders. She makes me cups of weak tea, which I detest but drink anyway. Once she even loads my dishwasher. I feel ashamed, but not too ashamed to stop her.

I don't even watch much TV. Mostly I just lie on the sofa and stare out. One day I look up to see Susan's son outside my window. He's just standing there on the lawn, staring at the hedge. A cabbage-white butterfly flaps around his head; he flaps it away. It continues to draft around him in lazy circles. Half-hypnotised, I watch – suddenly his hand lashes out and grabs it. He turns around, fist to his mouth. His eyes are blank and mild. *He hasn't?* – I think, repelled, then, with a quick shock – *he has!* His fist drops to his side and he smiles, widely. There is a pale smudge on his cheek.

'Tony! Tony!' It is Susan. She scuttles out onto my lawn, worn sandals slapping against her feet. I see her grab her son's arm and whisper agitatedly in his ear. She scans the houses, up, down, quickly before they disappear inside. For the next week or so I don't see Tony again. Only the *crunch-crunch* of gravel on bin day reminds me of his presence.

One day I hear Tom and his wife – Mary, I think her name is, but I'm not sure – have a fight. It's the middle of the day and all the cars are gone. I hear their voices raised and loud. *Lucky John's not here.* I smile. A bicycle helmet sails through the air to land on the drive. I jump. Her voices comes in patches of noise, like radio waves. '…how can you…never here…live here anymore!' Her voice climbs higher. '…For God's sake!' I listen, hopefully, but don't hear any more. Later, Tom walks by with the dog and quietly scoops the cycle helmet from the gravel path.

Finally, I see the famous outlaws from the other end of the estate. When they appear I am drinking one of Maureen's revolting cups of tea. I don't see them at first, but hear Maureen's soft intake of breath. I look up. They strut down the cul-de-sac, legs apart, a slight roll to their steps. They're both wearing dirty tracksuits, the bottoms tucked into thick white socks. One of them is bare-chested. Both have cropped hair, scowling faces and elaborate tattoos. They saunter slowly, insolently, staring from side to side.

'Don't worry,' I say to Maureen. 'They're only kids.

They're only about Tony's age.' One of the boys has picked up a ball, presumably belonging to Tom's young son. He arches his back and flings it over the wall, into the next street. Maureen looks away. They kick a stone up and down then, bored, leave.

Now that I have seen them once, they become a regular presence. I can usually hear them shouting before I see them, hard, guttural voices. They seem permanently angry, or maybe that's just due to the cans of Dutch Gold in their hands. Mostly they swear at each other, or listen to loud rap music on their phones. They seem bored, irritated with each other, but unable to separate. They can't see me in my darkened room, but I can see them, and count their small crimes. One dull afternoon, they throw cans at the cherry tree, trying to knock off the blossom. The petals shower down to their whooping cries. I am tense with rage. So is John when he drives home to see the cans scattered over the drive. 'Shocking,' he says. 'Something needs to be done.'

I can even tell the boys apart now. One is blonde, perpetually bare-chested, or wearing a low-cut white vest, all the better to show off this body art. Most of his chest is covered with an Irish flag. His arms ripple with Celtic symbols. An eagle caws on his ribcage. The other boy is dark-haired, with a low monobrow drawn in a tight, permanent scowl. He always wears sports tops and sports heavy jewellery, his hands studded with large gold rings. Maureen no longer cleans my windows, or even her own. She stays inside. When the boys appear, I hear her turn her TV up louder, as if to drown out the sight of them. We all stay inside.

One day Tony is cycling outside, turning in slow, careful circles on the path when they arrived. I can hear them calling to him, see them wave beckoning arms. They give him an open can. He drinks, splutters, looks confused. They are laughing, amused, nasty.

'Hey!' I knock on the window. Tony looks at me. 'Come here Tony, I need you to take out the bin.' His face clears, he hands the can back and walks over. The boys jeer –'Jaysus, she has ya whipped,' one calls. The other walks closer and jabs his middle finger at me. A large ring with a marijuana-leaf insignia glints in the sunlight. 'Ya want anythin' else doin', missus?' he calls insolently. I ignore them and close the door. Tony makes for the bin.

'It's fine,' I say. 'Actually I don't think the bin is full enough to go out. Would you like some biscuits instead?' He nods eagerly. Later, I walk him back to Susan's, and tell her what happened. Her hand flutters to her mouth in distress. 'Don't worry,' I say reassuringly. 'You might just want to keep him away from them. They're pretty low characters.'

The next day, they're back, and ugly, ready for reprisal. They claw handfuls out of my lawn and throw them at the windows. The clods smear, brown and sticky on the panes. I retreat to the kitchen at the back. My heart is thumping. I make myself sit down, and breathe deeply until I stop shaking. *Calm down,* I tell myself savagely. The phone rings. I'm glad of the distraction.

'Hello?'

'Hello.' The voice is quivery. 'This is Susan. Are you alright?'

'I am.' I say. 'Those guys are back though – they threw mud at my house.'

She makes a clucking sound. 'I know, I can see them. One of them is... *weeing* on the tree. Shall I ring the guards?'

'Do that. Good idea. Thanks.' I put the phone down.

When the gardai arrive, they are two young men, who clearly think we have exaggerated the whole incident. I inspect the damage as Susan gives them the details. She points at me, at the sale sign, the tree. My windows are filthy with dirt. Maureen appears by my side.

'I'll help you tidy up.'

'Thanks.' I am distracted. A branch has been broken off the beautiful cherry tree. The sale sign from next door has been broken in two halves and flung across my lawn. In the middle of it all, John comes home. He gets out of the car, face white with fury.

'Guards! Vandalism!' He sees the sale sign. His hands pump themselves into fists. 'For God's sake! I'll need to get on to the agent. What if someone is coming to view the house? Tony!' Tony appears. 'Good lad, get a bin-bag, clear up that branch and the sign. Where's Tom? Get him to do something with the lawn.' He is breathing heavily. Maureen reaches a timid hand to his sleeve. He swats off her frail hand. 'They won't get away with this. I need to call an emergency meeting of the Neighbourhood Watch.' He spits out the name viciously as he slams the door of his house. I hear him, faintly, as he shouts on the phone.

It is the last we see of the outlaws. Maybe it is the presence of the gardai that does it. Maybe it is the new Neighbourhood Watch patrols that circle the block in the afternoons. Within days the cul-de-sac begins to resume its normal, day-to-day life. I start walking every morning. Soon I will be ready to go back to school. It's almost summer. Sean has decided I will only supervise exams, a slow lead-in to full engagement with the job. I tell Tom I am ready to start mowing my own lawn again, and give him a bottle of whisky as a thank you. Tony still insists on taking out my bins. Susan dismisses my protestations. 'You were good to him when those boys came for him.' A new sale sign has appeared on the lawn next door. I see Maureen sweeping the path in front of the empty house, probably on John's orders. I call to her, but she ducks her head down. For some reason she is avoiding me. I am persistent; invite her in for afternoon tea. She sits and nibbles at sandwiches, saying little. I return to the topic of the vandalism.

'Tom has done wonders to my lawn. You'd never guess those idiots had torn it up.' She opens her mouth, and then closes it again.

'What is it?' Maureen sits back, and shakes her head.

'Nothing.' Her voice is a whisper. I give up and pour the tea.

The house next door has been sold. 'For more than the asking price!' John is incandescent, delighted. 'We're grand now.' He plans drinks to celebrate, insisting we have them the next day. 'As long as there's no litter left afterwards,' says Tom, with a grin. Mary (it is Mary) laughs and looks at him fondly. Everyone seems lighter, happier. The hooligans have gone, peace is restored and the house is sold. 'Sold to a barrister!' John could not be happier. He organises the party like a military expedition. I am allotted to bring ice. I give in to the feeling of festivity.

The next day, the sun is shining. Everyone is dressed up,

smiling, relieved. I see them as I set off for my usual walk. I stroll out of the estate down to the river. I breathe in the smell, the warm, green smell of sun on grass. The ground is mulch from the light rain; it is springy underfoot. I watch my pink Converse sneakers walk, sure and confident, on the brown and green of the soil. On my way back, it looks like it is going to rain again. I quicken my steps. Suddenly I stop. I see something gleam gold in the gravel of our road. I pick it up, and stare. In my hand is a ring, an ugly, brassy ring. I close my fingers around it. The stupid marijuana leaf insignia imprints itself on my palm. I curl my hands into wet knots of fingers.

I look from it to the estate, at the vista of neat little red-brick houses, at Tom's dog, nuzzling Tony's hand, as Tony laughs in glee. Susan and Maureen are laying out glasses on the trestle table.

I look back. The black outline of the leaf stands out against my skin; clearer, truer and more horrifying than anything I'd imagined. I feel my heart, jolt, shudder, and then beat jackhammer-hard in my chest.

John waves me over. 'Good day, isn't it?' I nod, cold with creeping realisation.

'We look after each other, don't we?' Wet lips peel back bared in a grin. His teeth are long and yellow. My arms ripple with gooseflesh. 'We all look after each other here. It's a lovely place to live.'

I LOOK LIKE YOU. I SPEAK LIKE YOU. I WALK LIKE YOU.

Have you ever seen someone who looks *just* like you? It's a terrifying moment. For a second, in front of you, is a replica, with your eyes, your hair, and your gestures. Usually you blink and stare, and then realise that the resemblance isn't so great after all. The eye colour is different, after all, she's fatter than you, when she smiles her teeth are large and overlapping.

But what if you met someone who looked *exactly* like you? What if you had a double? Someone who looked just like you, but was better, better in every way.

Sometimes it's hard to tell what's happened from what's happening. When I think back, it's difficult to remember; all gaps and images and fragments like slivers of broken glass. Our lives are like a series of overlapping tracks as our stories overspill into the lives of others. Everything exists at once, and, paradoxically, not at all. In my head, past and present slew around in my head, small, sharp fragments of unfinished stories.

On my lap there is a biscuit tin. It's a faded box of Danish butter cookies. I know he won't look there. He hates those cookies, complaining they taste like margarine. My legacy is in here. The worn and dented tin contains all about me that has survived. In it are a few old photos and faded clippings. When everything is quiet at night, I come down here, to the damp-smelling kitchen of the apartment, and pull the biscuit tin out from under the sink. I take out a photograph, carefully. This is my most precious possession, a photograph of us. It's black and creamy yellowish-white and creased around the edges. At one point it must have been folded in two – a cracked seam runs down the image, dividing our solemn, curly heads, our fat little arms around each other's waists.

When I close my eyes I picture us like this, twinned and

embryo-close, secure within our black and white bubble. I see our one true tale diverge and splinter into fractured narratives. Susieandstella. Susie. Stella.

We were happy then. I remember our dolls – twins too – with their flaxen hair and marble-blue eyes. We would push them in two tiny prams, heads together like gossipy married women, endlessly babbling.

Sometimes when I look in the mirror, I see her, our mother. I see the tired fear in her eyes. I think of her as we last saw her, on the kitchen floor, her face a pulp of blood and bone. She reached out to me. *'My babies.'* I turned and ran and hid with you, bodies pressed tight in the kind darkness of the airing cupboard. The hot water tank shuddered and hiccupped beside us as we hid, silent, for a long time, holding hands, mute. I can still remember how much the light hurt my eyes when the unfamiliar people opened the door.

When they took you away, I cried so much I was sick. I was in a strange house with unfamiliar smells and a hard bed. Kind people tried to get me to tell them what my favourite food was. I just turned my face and wept until my face was sticky and swollen. I wouldn't talk. Not one word. *In deep shock,* I heard one nurse tell another at the hospital. I just wanted you back, my sister, myself; your small arms tight around me at night. I often wonder who the expert was who recommended we be parted. It doesn't happen like that anymore, you know. They try everything to keep siblings together.

Then one, by one, the years ticked by, and when I was old enough to find you, you had already disappeared.

I met him at a fairground on the edge of the city. I was there with some friends, wandering around, enjoying the swell of music and the smell of candy floss mingling with the hot, iron perfume of the machines. My friend Karen knew him from work. They were talking about something, laughing together. I was watching a ride with narrowed eyes, wondering if I had the courage to get on it. It was a row of little boat-carriages for two that swung around recklessly from side to side, threatening to, but never quite, turning over.

I watched it, intent on the screaming, joyous faces of the riders swirling by me.

'Are you scared?' His low voice came from behind me, his breath tickling my neck.

I shivered, excited, nervous.

'I think I can do it.'

He smiled at me. His teeth were large and perfectly white. 'I know you can'. He flicked my arm lightly. His hands were large and immaculate, strong and long-fingered. We looked at each other.

'Harry,' he said.

'Stella.'

The ride had finished. We continued to stand, inches apart.

'I'll go with you.' He scooped me up like a grocery bag and dropped me into the nearest carriage. The little boat rocked as he climbed in, swaying hard under his weight. His thigh was taut against mine. My heart was beating in my throat, in a delightful panic.

I can still feel the imprint of his large hands on my body, his confident touch, his fingers firm and assured.

Last month it was my wrist.

'Fuckin' BITCH!'

He pushed me over, hard. By the time I hit the worn linoleum of the floor I was already crying, my stomach clenched in fear. It was almost a relief to feel the sick pain in my wrist and to hear myself scream. It was enough for him, I could see it. His mouth was already stretching at the sides into a hard grimace that tried to be a smile. He stood over me and his hands dropped to his sides.

Sometimes I see them. Others like me. Once when I was waiting, arm limp in my lap, aching head pressed against the damp, green walls of A&E I saw one watching me. She was holding a bloody rag to her face. One eye was a puffed and bleeding mess. But the other looked straight at me. In her one eye I saw reflected the sick resignation in my own. *I am just like you,* her steady gaze said. I closed my eyes. When I opened them she was gone.

If this wasn't my story, if some unfortunate woman were

telling it to me, I'd laugh. I would. I'd laugh and say: *Walk out the door! Just leave him!* It's impossible to describe the death of hope to free people, those invisible barriers that spring up, around the house, around your behaviour. You just don't know what it's like.

It grinds you down, as one tense day follows another, like beads on a string. Once I bought the wrong milk, semi-skimmed instead of full fat. They'd changed the colour of the carton, you see, and I hadn't noticed. But he did. I remember the cold light of the fridge glowing blue-white as he turned around, and the warm, helpless trickle of urine that ran down my leg as I saw his face.

It's the waiting that's the worst bit. The wondering. Is the flat clean enough for his inspection? Will he be alright when he comes in? If I stay up, will he hit me for nagging? If I go to bed, will he come and get me? He's done it a few times, you see, grabbed me by the ankles and pulled me out. Once I went flying down the stairs. That was the worst. That was the time the doctor could barely look at me, she was so sick with disgust at my pathetic improvised story as he stood over me, breathing heavily, watching, listening.

I finger my lip, almost unconsciously. There's a thin line down it, from when he split it last year. It was one of the first times he hit me, and I suppose he wasn't practiced enough. I remember his consternation.

'God! I'm sorry! Here, mop it up. Should I get a plaster?' His face was suddenly anxious, hovering above mine. I lay on the floor, dazed. I felt my lip swell and throb, the blood bubbling over it and into my mouth. I remember him dabbing at it, a hot wet cloth with the pungent smell of Dettol.

'You fell over,' he says. 'It could happen to anyone.' I close my eyes and weakly, horribly, enjoy the soft touch of cloth on my lip, his anxious hands cradling my face.

If you leave me, I'll kill you. Killing me is his answer for so many things. Going to the police. Complaining. Making trouble. Spilling tea.

I don't work. Of course I don't work. How would I explain the on-off limping, the bruises on the arm, the wincing as I sit down? Nor do I have friends. Having friends carries a penalty, judiciously exacted. Friends are a threat to him, you see. There was Maura, a nice Irish girl I'd met in the park near the flats. She rang the house phone once. He answered the phone, hung up, and then punched me methodically once, twice, hard in the stomach.

'I told you,' he said, his voice is almost regretful. 'No calls.'

I see my death written in his face. It will happen some night when he's just that bit too drunk, when he hits just that bit too hard, and those huge hands that once held me in love will punch me out of this life.

In the end it wasn't so hard to find you, Susie. For some reason I thought it would be a lot more difficult. I remember worrying about not having enough money to hire a private detective, but there are agencies, kind, concerned agencies set up to help you track down relatives lost through fostering. My twin story went down well; the dog-eared photograph never failed to elicit a cry of sympathy.

I've found you now. We live in the same city, but on different sides. I know your name, where you live. I stalk you on Facebook. I see what you like. Heartwarming stories about dogs found and restored to their owners. We have the same face, the same body, but your life is different in every possible way. I watch the video of your birthday party, uploaded to YouTube. I see the unconscious flutter of your right hand to your lips when surprised. I do that too. I learn everything about you. I want to know it all, to develop the same likes and dislikes. I want to know who your friends are. I want to know your jokes, your recurring spelling mistakes and your favourite dress. There are so many things to learn before we can meet. When it happens it has to be picture-perfect.

When he hits me I freeze. I hug my body in my arms, but even as I cry and beg and plead, even as I shrink from his terrible fists, I withdraw. In my head it's is already over. I think of you, my sweet sister, I think of you in your shiny home, your family nestled around you like baby chicks in a straw basket.

Your life is so flawless. I watch it in the dim light of my laptop, while he snores drunkenly upstairs. Your house is large and colourful. Your husband has a fat, kind face with dark, guileless eyes. He has dimples on his cheeks as he hugs the girls. Your two little girls, Pearl and Veronica. Old-fashioned, hipster names. I touch their rosy faces on the cold screen.

If locating you was exciting, it's nothing compared to the anxiety and delight of meeting you for the first time in twenty-five years. My palms are sweaty as I wait in the anonymous café on a side-street, carefully chosen to be at a safe distance from my house or yours. I see you first; I see you walk in, look around. Your face reflects my own confused and fearful excitement. When I see you walk towards me, I feel my heart stutter in my chest; it pulses in the hot pain of emotion. *I look like you. I speak like you. I walk like you. I am you.* But I'm not you.

You see me. 'Stella?' you say uncertainly. Even my voice is yours, yours is mine.

I nod. Words are beyond me. You put your hand to my face, tracing the scar on my lip. Your eyes are full of tears. When I hug you, it is like holding a warm mirror. Face to face, belly to belly. Together we fit like soft Lego, neat and tight. Your arms give the tight comfort, I remember.

I show you the crumpled black and white photograph and your eyes widen. *How wonderful,* you breathe, touching it lightly with your fingertips.

Susie. Susie. Susie.

I like my own face more now I've met you. You look so pretty.

I cut my hair like yours. It costs me a beating. I don't mind. I have started to look in mirrors again. I am surprised how normal I look. Except for the faint lip-scar and the wariness in my eyes, I could be you. I compare myself to the Facebook selfies of you, my sister-double, and I am pleased. I hug you to myself like a precious secret. I buy myself a mobile phone. If he finds it, he will be incandescent. It would be construed as evidence of my having friends, informing on him, planning to leave him. We text each other; the texts are our memories made concrete. *We had a doll called Lucy. Remember that? She wet herself. We didn't like her.* My phone lives in the biscuit tin. I retrieve it and read these words over and over in the darkness of the night.

I have a new courage now. For the first time in years I feel I am awake. I can feel everything more vividly, the heat of the sun on my forearms, the smell of warm flesh that rises from them. I wear heels. Mascara. Once I wore red lipstick but he smacked my mouth so hard my lip broke open again. I learned.

We meet the next day. 'What happened to your lip?' Your voice is soft with concern.

'Oh,' I say. 'It's just a bit of blood. I tripped and fell on the way home. I'm sure my lip will heal soon.'

'It looks,' you swallow, 'like someone hit you.' You look directly at me. 'Promise me that isn't true.'

I look back in your eyes. My gaze is open, honest. 'Of course not!' In a way, I'm not lying. When I am with you, the scared, small version of me falls away. It is only with an effort that I can remember my old life, waiting for me at the end of every meeting, the end of every day.

You leave this line of enquiry but I can still see a fleck of doubt in your eyes. Maybe I can only see it because I know what they look like so well; I have seen them in the grip of every emotion I have ever had.

'You haven't told your family yet, have you?' I ask.

'No,' you say, grudgingly. 'But I want to tell Tom.' Tom is her childish-looking husband, with the smile and the puppy-fat.

'Not yet,' I say. 'There's so much to take in. Everyone will be so surprised. Harry doesn't even know I have a twin.'

Your face clears. 'Me neither. I was feeling so guilty, talking to you. It's just–' you lower your head '–still painful to remember.'

I cover your hand with mine. Both our hands are thin and pale, with fingernails that curve slightly over, like talons. Even our wedding bands mirror each other. 'I know,' I say. 'Let's start tomorrow evening. I'll break the news to Harry tonight. You come over afterwards. We'll see how it goes. Then tomorrow night, we'll both go home and tell Tom.'

#

I don't tell Harry anything. Instead I wait for him to leave in the morning. I open the biscuit tin and take out the phone. The photograph I tuck into my bra. It's not a perfect fit, but the edges are so worn and creased that they lie soft against my skin.

I go downstairs and get to work. First I open the fridge. I sweep everything out, onto the floor. Milk spills, meat splatters bloodily, yoghurt cartons burst. I take the eggs out of their carton and smash them, one by one, against the cupboards I have spent my life polishing. I break the dishes. That is a lot of fun. I throw the rose-patterned dinner service his mother bought us against the wall. They smash beautifully, their shards glinting in the sun-shafts from the window.

When I am finished I go upstairs. I stuff the toilet with paper, and then flush it till it overflows. I take the kitchen scissors and saw through the down pillows and duvet. A stream of feathers fall and drift around my head, like an illicit snowdrift. I am breathing heavily now, heart beating in a queer mixture of fear and exhilaration.

When I am finished, I take a long bath, dress in my most anonymous black dress, and climb into the wardrobe of the spare room.

When he comes home, his rage is huge, electrifying. He roars my name all over the house. Underneath my layer of coats, I cower, afraid that his anger will lend him a super-human sensory ability to find me. I can hear him shout and throw things downstairs, then finally, the weighty slap of his feet as he climbs the stairs.

'STELLA!' I am so silent I can hear his panting as he walks up and down the corridor. 'If you're here, I'll kill you.' I hear the sound of the bed in my room as it's flung to one side. 'If you're hiding here, I'll kill you slowly, I swear to God.' Now comes a heavy thud as something (the chest of drawers?) hits the floor.

He calls from the next room. 'Are you in the wardrobe?' I stiffen in fear. *Keep away from the guest room ward-robe!* I think, alarmed. I hadn't expected him to search so thoroughly.

'Helloooooo,' he calls, then slams my wardrobe door shut. 'If you're not here, I'll find you and kill you anyway.' I shrink down further and further into the pile of old coats, drawing my knees close to my chin. If he finds me, this is all over.

The doorbell pings.

Right on time.

His feet are thumping down the stairs, an angry tattoo. He is swearing, his voice heavy and ugly in his throat. The door scrapes back, then slams shut. Her voice squawks, pleads. He is on her. I crouch low in the wardrobe, my hands over my ears, but I can still hear it. The screaming, the roars, the hard, repeated slamming against the wall, his fist, her face, I don't know which. I press the preset number on my phone and listen to the ringing. 'Come quickly,' I whisper. 'It's next door, No. 25 Chalforth Road. Come quick!'

I press the button to hang up.

'Stella, you stupid bitch.' His voice is nearer now; I hear the scrabble of her heels against the floor. He is dragging her in the hallway. Her voice is thick and slurred. 'M'm not... not her...' He doesn't listen. There is another horrific, hard thump of flesh on flesh, then a final thud, a slip-slide of a body coming to rest. I peek out of the wardrobe and see you, head bent at an impossible angle, eyes wide and staring. I am glad you can't see me. He is on his knees, his back to me, crying, his bloody hands clasped around his head.

'You stupid bastard,' I murmur in a low, unemotional voice, and walk by, walk lightly out of this house like I have always dreamed of.

I pause going out the door. One last thing. I take the razor blade out of my bag.

I open the door and hang up my coat. The kitchen door opens.

'What happened to your face?'

'It's just a bit of blood. I tripped and fell on the way home. I'm sure my lip will heal soon. I've hurt my wrist a bit too.' I extend my swollen hand.

His face is soft and slightly pudgy, eyes dark with compassion.

'Poor thing,' he says. 'You're home now. I'll look after you.' His fingers touch my face gently. I flinch. 'Would you like to go to A&E now?'

I shake my head. 'Not right now. I'm a little worn out from the shock of it all. I'll just lie down for a bit.'

Once we were identical. We had curls and held hands. Our mother gathered us to her soft body. The world was new and full of love.

I watch my precious photograph crinkle and burn, our baby faces twisting and melting in the flames. You will always be with me, my dark twin, forever inside me. It was more than the lip scar, you see. It was all the scars, countless, invisible, internal. The scars that covered my love for you in a thick crust like crocodile skin. Now I'm cold. I'm hard. I'll do anything to get out. Same city, different sides.

I look like you. I speak like you. I walk like you.

But I'm not you.

LOOKING FOR WILDGOOSE
LODGE

It's 2012. I'm standing on a hill with a rough stone in my hand and tears drying cold on my face. I'm finally here, in this strange space that has haunted me for so long.

It's 1979. I'm lying in bed, the caterpillar ridges of the pink candlewick bedspread tickling my nose. The red rear-lights of my parents' car wash through the thin curtains, casting an ominous red glow on the walls. The door opens a crack. My grandmother's curly head is silhouetted against the hall light.

'You'll want a story then?' We both know that this is a rhetorical question.

'Yes,' I say happily. The bed creaks under her weight.

'Well now,' she says (and by her voice I can tell she is smiling). 'What story do you want?'

I ponder the choices. Her stories are a rich cornucopia of possibilities. There's the Curse of the Four Fs, St Mochta's Cell, the Jumping Church, the Cracked Grave... I consider the options and choose – 'Wildgoose Lodge, please Granny.'

It's 1999. I'm sitting in the hospital beside my grandmother's bed. A busy nurse hurries by.

'Nearly time for her to rest,' she says, but gently. Everyone is gentle in the intensive care ward. In fact, my grandmother is almost asleep. Her eyelids flutter and droop, jerk open, then droop slowly back down again. We hold hands. Her hand is no longer the plump, work-roughened one mine remembers; it is smaller, shrunken, harder. Her eyelids fall shut. I gather up my handbag and ease my hand out of hers. Instantly her eyes flicker open.

'Don't go.' Her voice is so low that the hum of the machines behind her almost drowns it out. I settle back in the chair.

'I'm not going anywhere,' I say, in what I hope is my most reassuring voice. I put my bag firmly back down on the worn linoleum of the floor and place my hand back on hers.

There's a double-bleep from a nearby monitor. Another nurse pauses to check the readings.

'You know what?' I say. 'I'll tell you a story. Any story you like.'

It's 1979. My grandmother draws a dramatic breath and starts the story. 'The Lynch family lived in a house called Wildgoose Lodge,' she began. 'Now this is a true story and it all happened just up the road. But, long ago, there was a wicked bunch of soldiers – the Brits – who wanted to get rid of this family. So, the soldiers met in a church and, in front of the altar, they took a vow to kill them all. So off they went that night, in the dark, and they surrounded the Lodge. They lit it all on fire, and the flames danced around, lighting up the countryside. People started gathering, the way people do when there's a fire, but no one did anything.' Her voice rose sharply, as it always did at this point. 'Inside the family were burning and screaming, but no one helped them. The wife tried to save her youngest child, a baby. She broke a window and held the baby out, but a soldier raised his bayonet, stuck it through the baby, and threw it back into the fire saying, "Nits make lice."'

In the darkness, I feel the familiar, cold wriggle of horror in my stomach. It's a horrible story. I don't know why I ask for it. But I'm mesmerised by its awfulness. For a minute we are suspended in a bubble of silence and darkness as we contemplate the fire and screams.

'No good came to any of them after,' she says quietly. 'The ringleader Devan was caught and hanged, and so was half the neighbourhood, guilty and innocent alike.' My grandmother's stories are laced with death. Few characters survive. She takes another breath. 'Even the great homes connected with it died out, the four families whose names began with F, they all fell victim to the curse of the Four F's.'

'And this really happened?' I ask, as I always do.

'It did, and just down the road, in Wildgoose Lodge.'

This is the final line. She gets up and closes the door. I lie in the dark imagining the terrible heat of the Lodge, the faceless men, the spitted baby.

I don't think my parents really knew about the stories she

told me.

It's 1988. I'm bored, and in the reference section of the local library. It is the Year of the Leaving Certificate – that dreaded entity of multiple school examinations. I'm meant to be revising for a chemistry exam, according to my revision planner, but my desk is recklessly piled with odd books, novels, poetry, stories. I suck my pen, rolling it about my mouth in an expert fashion, like a sailor with a hand-rolled cigarette, as I read. Idly, I flip through the pages of the *Penguin Book of Irish Short Stories*, and then stop. There it is. Wildgoose Lodge, by William Carleton. *Surely not*, I think, disturbed, *not Granny's Lodge?* Confused, I suck furiously at the pen until I taste bitter ink on my tongue and spit it out. It is the same Wildgoose Lodge. I'm enchanted. The ominous, multi-coloured revision planner lies beside me, utterly forgotten. Here they are, my old acquaintances, the Lynch family. There are no soldiers though. The soldiers are, in fact, Irish Ribbonmen. *Strange*, I wonder, *was it easier to cast the English soldiers as the villains?* For a minute, my faith in Granny's story falters then is restored as I read on. The familiar script picks up from its momentary lull to move seamlessly through the old set-pieces – the trip through the dark fields, the old Lodge aflame. I read on, breathlessly, as the poor Lynches, trapped in their terrible narrative, once again re-enact their final moments. The desperate mother thrusts the child forward, the captain stabs his bayonet, and utters the words: '*Your child is a coal now,' said he, with deliberate mockery.*' For a second I hear my grandmother's narrative, see the soldier silhouetted against the fire, the baby piked at the end of his bayonet. I feel a perfect shock, like ice-water down my back, despite the dusty warmth of the library.

I check the date of the story. 1833. For years I'd contemplated that dark circle of surrounding faces, unmoved and unmoving, lit by the red flames of the Lodge. The date finally answers the dreadful question I had never dared to ask my grandmother – 'Were you there?'

It's 2012. I've spent over an hour trying to find the site of Wildgoose Lodge. I'm armed with a copy of the Carleton story and my grandmother's imprecise description – 'just down the road.' My aunt, when I call her, proves a more reliable source, directing me through a complex series of manoeuvres down roads and laneways, with a suggestion to ask for final directions at a nearby farmhouse. As I drive I realise that this place, this strange place, is only half a mile down the road from my grandmother's house. Her directions are more correct that I had thought.

I get out of the car and rap on the farmhouse door. Silence. Then a dog barks, once, twice, and then there is a steady staccato burst of barking from the backyard. I'm rehearsing my lines, but when the door finally opens I just blurt out, 'I'm looking for Wildgoose Lodge.'

There's a pause as the stout woman in the doorway looks at me carefully.

'Aye?' She clearly needs more information.

'I'm Alice Moore's granddaughter,' I explain. 'She told me the story when I was very young. I've always wondered where it happened.'

Her expression softens. 'Alice Moore! She was a lovely woman. I thought for a minute you were one of those history people that come here wanting to rake it all up again. It was a bad business. Some things should be let lie.'

'Sorry,' I say instinctively.

'You're grand,' she says dismissively. 'You're local, that's different.'

She stands beside me and points to her right.

'Just up that track and it's on top of the hill.' She stops to consider something. 'Sure I'll walk up a bit of the way with you. I have to go up to the cows anyway.' Picking up a bucket from the doorway, she nods at me. We walk up the lane. I feel suddenly, absurdly nervous. She chats on – the weather, the growing shortness of the days, the rise in petrol prices. I don't listen, distracted by the welling bubble of anxiety in my stomach.

We turn the corner. She points again. 'There it is.' I look and see a huge tree, darkly silhouetted against the sky, an uneven scrub of grass and hedge surrounding it.

'It looks like a fairy fort,' I say, marvelling.

'It's one of those type of places alright.'

I look confused.

'One of those places, you know, ones people don't go

near.'

'I know what you mean.'

She sighs. 'Maybe it was a fairy fort once. Places like that do get used again and again. Bad places.' She hefts the bucket from one arm to the other. 'I'll not go up there with you. Take care, Alice's granddaughter.'

'Thanks,' I say. I can't take my eyes off the towering tree.

But where is the Lodge? I walk towards the tree and clump of bushes. I can see fence posts surrounding the bushes, a slim strand of wire connecting them. I walk around, puzzled. Then I notice that, behind the wire, overgrown with leaves, are crumbling stone walls. I bend down and touch the stones. My heart thumps hard in my throat with sudden agitation. I run my fingers over the wall, the rough stone grazing my fingertips. In the distance the farm dog begins to bark, then stops abruptly. I'm silent, so silent I can hear my own breathing. For a moment, nothing exists except the texture of stone, this physical reality of a story. *My poor Lynches*, I think, *poor doomed little baby*. I pick up a stray stone and slowly straighten up. My eyes trace the pitiful ruin of the walls, hidden by bushes, overshadowed by the spreading branches of the tree. I can't believe the dimensions of this tiny lodge, the Lodge that has always stood so tall in my memories. I swallow hard.

It's 1992. I know what has happened. I know as soon as I step off the bus, my father's face tells me. When we open the car boot to stow our college rucksacks in the back, I see it, her little, battered, maroon suitcase that I once borrowed for a school trip to the Gaeltacht. It contains, my father confirms, her 'effects'. I look at it, my throat swelling with a football-sized ache. How can someone whose life was so large and unforgettable come to be contained in something so little? Years later, that suitcase will be one of the saddest things I remember.

It's 2012. I'm standing on a hill, with a rough stone in my hand, and tears drying cold on my face. I think of my grandmother, of her suitcase, of the tiny lodge. I'm crying for my sweet-sting memories, for time's terrible diminishment, for what remains behind when the story has ended.

Tracy Fahey writes short fiction that is concerned with ideas of uncanny domestic space and its various intersections with literature, art and folk-tales. Since taking up fiction writing in 2013, she has had short stories accepted for publication in anthologies by US and UK presses including Fox Spirit Press, Hic Dragones Press, Dark Minds Press, A Murder of Storytellers, Crystal Lake Publishing and Hydra Publications. *The Unheimlich Manoeuvre* ia her debut collection. Read more about her at her author website at www.designingtracy.wix.com/tracyfahey.

In her other life, as Dr. Tracy Fahey, where she runs a post-graduate department, a research centre and an art collective, she also writes academic articles on the Gothic published in collections by Routledge, Palgrave, Manchester University Press, McFarland, Rowman and Littlefield and Cork University Press.

ACKNOWLEDGEMENTS

These stories were written in scraps of time, on planes, trains, late at night and early in the morning, so it's particularly lovely to see them gathered together here, my uncanny offspring. Special thanks to my patient editor Alex Davis for working with me on this collection and to Care Gardner for writing her generous introduction. I'm indebted to past editors especially Hannah Kate, Adele Wearing, K.A. Laity, Ross Warren and Adrean Messmer for their encouragement, and to my invaluable beta readers, Tara, Scott and Brona.

Finally, thank you to you, the reader, for picking up this book and I trust that its *unheimlich* shadows won't return to haunt you...

COPYRIGHT ACKNOWLEDGEMENTS

Several of these stories have been published previously. Two of these have been published with Hic Dragones Press: 'Looking for Wildgoose Lodge' in *Impossible Spaces* (2013, Hic Dragones Press) and 'Ghost Estate Phase II', in *Hauntings* (2014, Hic Dragones Press). 'Coming Back' was published in *Girl At The End Of The World* (2014, Fox Spirit Press). 'Long Shadows' was published in *Where Dreams and Visions Live* (2014, CreateSpace), 'I Look Like You, I Speak Like You, I Walk Like You' in *Jotters United Litzine*, Issue 10 and 'Walking the Borderlines' in *Darkest Minds* (2015, Dark Minds Press). Other short stories are unique to this collection, including 'Papering Over The Cracks', 'Two Faced', 'Sealed', 'Perfect Pitch', 'The Woman Next Door,' and 'A Lovely Place To Live'.